A Dickens Christmas

COLLECTION

Harold Shaw Publishers
Wheaton, Illinois

ISBN 0-87788-170-7

Cover and inside design © 1995 by David LaPlaca

Compiled by Keith Call and Vinita Hampton Wright

Library of Congress Cataloging-in-Publication Data

Dickens, Charles, 1812-1870.
    A Dickens Christmas Collection [edited by Vinita Hampton Wright].
       p.   cm.
    ISBN 0-87788-170-7 (cloth)
    1. England—Social life and customs—19th century—fiction.
    2. Christmas stories, English.   I. Wright, Vinita Hampton, 1958- . II. Title.
    PR4557.A2W75 1995
    823'.8—dc20   95-30248
                                                          CIP

---

02 01 00 99 98 97 96 95

10 9 8 7 6 5 4 3 2

Contents

Christmas comes but once a year—
which is unhappily too true, for when it begins
to stay with us the whole year round
we shall make this earth a very different place.

—from "The Seven Poor Travellers"

Introduction

For this special collection we have chosen works by Charles Dickens that are specifically about Christmas, emphasizing the spiritual elements of the season. Spiritual elements are not difficult to find in Dickens, and their Christian origins are obvious. In this present day, when a changing culture demands that more and more of the spiritual Christmas be extracted from the Christmas season, we have made a point of demonstrating that Christmas would not exist without the Christ. Surely, Dickens considered this to be so.

Dickens's imaginative ponderings, his spiritual focus, his unique sensitivity to the welfare of people as he considered the meaning of the Christmas season—these are the things that make his holiday feasts a joy, his characters a triumph, and his themes continually new.

Our holiday centerpiece, *The Cricket on the Hearth* (an abridgment), with these other stories and excerpts are not tales we rush through for their information or their obvious messages. Rather, we read in order to participate in detailed memories, ones so deep and sweet that they demand a sigh, a familiar chair, and the accompaniment of good food and drink. As Dickens recalls the objects, the memories, and paradoxes that have evoked his wonder and praise, we have the opportunity to meander through the events of our own lives and Christmases—to be charmed and cheered by them again.

Chesterton
on
Dickens

G. K. Chesterton was well known as a reader and literary critic of Charles Dickens. From 1906–1909 he wrote a series of introductions to volumes of Dickens's works published by Everyman's Library.

Critics have called Keats and others who died young "the great Might-have-beens of literary history." Dickens certainly was not merely a great Might-have-been. Dickens, to say the least of him, was a great Was. Yet this fails fully to express the richness of his talent; for the truth is that he was a great Was and also a great Might-have-been. He said what he had to say, and yet not all he had to say. Wild pictures, possible stories, tantalizing and attractive trains of thought, perspectives of adventure, crowded so continually upon his mind that at the end there was a vast mass of them left over, ideas that he literally had not the opportunity to develop, tales that he literally had not the time to tell. This is shown clearly in his private notes and letters, which are full of schemes singularly striking and suggestive, schemes which he never carried out. It is indicated even more clearly by these *Christmas Stories,* collected out of the chaotic opulence of *Household Words* and *All the Year Round.** He wrote short stories actually because he had not time to write long stories. He often put into the short story a deep and branching idea which would have done very well for a long story; many of his long stories, so to speak, broke off short. This is where he differs from most who are called the Might-have-beens of literature.—*from the introduction to the* Christmas Stories

Dickens devoted his genius in a somewhat special sense to the description of happiness. No other literary man of his eminence has made this central human aim so specially his subject matter. Happiness is a mystery—generally a momentary mystery—which seldom stops long enough to submit itself to artistic observation, and which, even when it is habitual, has something about it which renders artistic description almost impossible. There are twenty tiny minor poets who can describe fairly impressively an eternity of agony; there are very few even of the eternal poets who can describe ten minutes of satisfaction. . . .

Human tradition, human custom and folk-lore (though far more true and reliable than literature as a rule) have not often succeeded in giving quite the correct symbols for a real atmosphere of *camaraderie* and joy. But here and there a note has been struck with the sudden vibration of the *vox humana*. In human tradition it has been struck chiefly in the old celebrations of Christmas. In literature it has been struck chiefly in Dickens's Christmas tales.—*from the introduction to the* Christmas Books

*Household Words was a weekly publication founded and edited by Dickens, first appearing in March 1850. Its purpose was "the raising up of those that are down, and the general improvement of our social condition." It was replaced in 1859 by *All the Year Round,* in which literary works, including *Great Expectations* and *A Tale of Two Cities* were serialized (*Charles Dickens: A December Vision and Other Thoughtful Writings,* p. 7–9).

A Christmas Dinner

(from *Sketches by Boz*)

*Reflect upon your present blessings—of which every man has many—
not your misfortunes, of which all men have some. Fill your glass
again, with a merry face and contented heart. Our life on it, but your
Christmas shall be merry, and your new year a happy one!*

Christmas Time! That man must be a misanthrope indeed, in whose breast something like a jovial feeling is not roused—in whose mind some pleasant associations are not awakened—by the recurrence of Christmas. There are people who will tell you that Christmas is not to them what it used to be; that each succeeding Christmas has found some cherished hope, or happy prospect, of the year before, dimmed or passed away; that the present only serves to remind them of reduced circumstances and straitened incomes—of the feasts they once bestowed on hollow friends, and of the cold looks that meet them now, in adversity and misfortune. Never heed such dismal reminiscences. There are few men who have lived long enough in the world, who cannot call up such thoughts any day in the year. Then do not select the merriest of the three hundred and sixty-five for your doleful recollections, but draw your chair nearer the blazing fire—fill the glass and send round the song—and if your room be smaller than it was a dozen years ago, or if your glass be filled with reeking punch, instead of sparkling wine, put a good face on the matter, and empty it off-hand, and fill another, and troll off the old ditty you used to sing, and thank God it's no worse. Look on the merry faces of your children (if you have any) as they sit round the fire. One little seat may be empty; one slight form that gladdened the father's heart, and roused the mother's pride to look upon, may not be there. Dwell not upon the past; think not that one short year ago, the fair child now resolving into dust, sat before you, with the bloom of health upon its cheek and the gaiety of infancy in its joyous eye. Reflect upon your present blessings—of which every man has many—not your misfortunes, of which all men have some. Fill your glass again, with a merry face and contented heart. Our life on it, but your Christmas shall be merry, and your new year a happy one!

Who can be insensible to the out-pourings of good feeling, and the honest interchange of affectionate attachment, which abound at this season of the year? A Christmas family-party! We know nothing in nature more delightful! There seems a magic in the very name of Christmas. Petty jealousies and discords are forgotten; social feelings are awakened, in bosoms to which they have long been strangers; father and son, or brother and sister, who have met and passed with averted gaze or a look of cold recognition, for months before, proffer and return the cordial embrace, and bury their past animosities in their present happiness. Kindly hearts that have yearned towards each other, but have been withheld by false notions of pride and self-dignity, are again reunited, and all is kindness and benevolence! Would that Christmas lasted the whole year through (as it ought), and that the prejudices and passions which deform our better nature, were never called into action among those to whom they should ever be strangers!

The Christmas family-party that we mean, is not a mere assemblage of relations, got up at a week or two's notice, originating this year, having no family precedent in the last, and not likely to be repeated in the next. No. It is an annual gathering of all the accessible members of the family, young or old, rich or poor; and all the children look forward to it, for two months beforehand, in a fever of anticipation. Formerly it was held at grandpapa's; but grandpapa getting old, and grandmamma getting old too, and rather infirm, they have given up housekeeping, and domesticated themselves with uncle George; so, the party always takes place at uncle George's house, but grandmamma sends in most of the good things, and grandpapa always *will* toddle down, all the way to Newgate-market, to buy the turkey, which he engages a porter to bring home behind him in triumph, always insisting on the man's being rewarded with a glass of spirits, over and above his hire, to drink "a merry Christmas and happy new year" to aunt George. As to grandmamma, she is very secret and mysterious for two or three days beforehand, but not sufficiently so to prevent rumours getting afloat that she has purchased a beautiful new cap with pink ribbons for each of the servants, together with sundry books, and pen-knives, and pencil-cases, for the younger branches; to say nothing of divers secret additions to the order originally given by aunt George at the pastry-cook's, such as another dozen of mince-pies for the dinner, and a large plum-cake for the children.

On Christmas-eve, grandmamma is always in excellent spirits, and after employing all the children during the day, in stoning the plums, and all that, insists, regularly every year, on uncle George coming down into the kitchen, taking off his coat, and stirring the pudding for half an hour or so, which uncle George good-humouredly does to the vociferous delight of the children and servants. The evening concludes with a glorious game of blind-man's buff, in an early stage of which grandpapa takes great care to be caught, in order that he may have an opportunity of displaying his dexterity.

On the following morning, the old couple, with as many of the children as the pew will hold, go to the church in great state: leaving aunt George at home dusting decanters and filling castors, and uncle George carrying bottles into the dining-parlour, and calling for corkscrews, and getting into everybody's way.

When the church-party return to lunch, grandpapa produces a small sprig of mistletoe from his pocket, and tempts the boys to kiss their little cousins under it—a proceeding which affords both the boys and the old gentleman unlimited satisfaction, but which rather outrages grandmamma's ideas of decorum, until grandpapa says, that when he was just thirteen years and three months old *he* kissed grandmamma under a mistletoe too, on which the children clap their hands, and laugh very heartily, as do aunt George and uncle George; and grandmamma looks pleased, and says, with a benevolent smile, that grandpapa was an impudent young dog, on which the children laugh very heartily again, and grandpapa more heartily than any of them.

But all these diversions are nothing to the subsequent excitement when grandmamma in a high cap, and slate-coloured silk gown; and grandpapa with a beautifully plaited shirt-frill, and white neckerchief; seat themselves on one side of the drawing-room fire, with uncle George's children and little cousins innumerable, seated in the front, waiting the arrival of the expected visitors. Suddenly a hackney-coach is heard to stop, and uncle George who has been looking out of the window, exclaims, "Here's Jane!" on which the children rush to the door, and helter-skelter down the stairs; and uncle Robert and aunt Jane, and the dear little baby, and the nurse, and the whole party, are ushered up stairs amidst tumultuous shouts of "Oh, my!" from the children, and frequently repeated warnings not to hurt the baby from the nurse. And grandpapa takes the child, and grandmamma kisses her daughter, and the confusion of this first entry has scarcely subsided, when some other aunts and uncles with more cousins arrive, and nothing is to be heard but a confused din of talking, laughing, and merriment.

A hesitating double knock at the street-door, heard during a momentary pause in the conversation, excites a general inquiry of "Who's that?" and two or three children, who have been standing at the window, announce in a low voice, that it's "poor aunt Margaret." Upon which, aunt George leaves the room to welcome the new comer; and grandmamma draws herself up, rather stiff and stately; for Margaret married a poor man without her consent, and poverty not being a sufficient weighty punishment for her offence, has been discarded by her friends, and debarred the society of her dearest relatives. But Christmas has come round, and the unkind feelings that have struggled against better dispositions during the year, have melted away before its genial influence, like half-formed ice beneath the morning sun. It is not difficult in a moment of angry feeling for a parent to denounce a disobedient child; but, to banish her at a period of general good will and hilarity, from the hearth, round which she has sat on so many anniversaries of the same day, expanding by slow degrees from infancy to girlhood, and then bursting, almost imperceptibly, into a woman, is widely different. The air of conscious rectitude, and cold forgiveness, which the old lady has assumed, sits ill upon her; and when the poor girl is led in by her sister, pale in looks and broken in hope—not from poverty, for that she could bear, but from the consciousness of undeserved neglect, and unmerited unkindness—it is easy to see how much of it is assumed. A momentary pause succeeds; the girl breaks suddenly from her sister and throws herself, sobbing, on her mother's neck. The father steps hastily forward, and takes her husband's hand. Friends crowd round to offer their hearty congratulations, and happiness and harmony again prevail.

As to the dinner, it's perfectly delightful—nothing goes wrong, and everybody is in the very best of spirits, and disposed to please and be pleased. Grandpapa relates a circumstantial account of the purchase of the turkey, with a slight digression relative to the purchase of previous turkeys, on former Christmas-days, which grandmamma corroborates in the minutest particular. Uncle George tells stories, and carves poultry, and takes wine, and jokes with the children at the side-table, and winks at the cousins, and exhilarates everybody with his good humour and hospitality; and when, at last, a stout servant staggers in with a gigantic pudding, with a sprig of holly in the top, there is such a laughing, and shouting, and clapping of little chubby hands, and kicking up of fat dumpy legs, as can only be equalled by the applause with which the astonishing feat of pouring lighted brandy into mince-pies, is received by the younger visitors. Then the dessert!—and the wine!—and the fun! Such beautiful speeches, and *such* songs, from aunt Margaret's husband, who turns out to be such a nice man, and *so* attentive to grandmamma! Even grandpapa not only sings his annual song with unprecedented vigour, but on being honoured with an unanimous *encore*, according to annual custom, actually comes out with a new one which nobody but grandmamma ever heard before; and a young scape-grace of a cousin, who has been in some disgrace with the old people, for certain heinous sins of omission and commission—neglecting to call, and persisting in drinking Burton ale—astonishes everybody into convulsions of laughter by volunteering the most extraordinary comic songs that ever were heard. And thus the evening passes, in a strain of rational goodwill and cheerfulness, doing more to awaken the sympathies of every member of the party in behalf of his neighbour, and to perpetuate their good feeling, during the ensuing year, than half the homilies that have ever been written, by half the Divines that have ever lived.

A Christmas Tree

Being now at home again, and alone, the only person in the house awake, my thoughts are drawn back, by a fascination which I do not care to resist, to my own childhood. I begin to consider, what do we all remember best upon the branches of the Christmas Tree of our own young Christmas days by which we climbed to real life.

I have been looking on, this evening, at a merry company of children assembled round that pretty German toy, a Christmas Tree. The tree was planted in the middle of a great round table, and towered high above their heads. It was brilliantly lighted by a multitude of little tapers; and everywhere sparkled and glittered with bright objects. There were rosy-cheeked dolls, hiding behind the green leaves; and there were real watches, (with movable hands, at least, and an endless capacity of being wound up) dangling from innumerable twigs; there were French-polished tables, chairs, bedsteads, wardrobes, eight-day clocks, and various other articles of domestic furniture (wonderfully made, in tin, at Wolverhampton), perched among the boughs, as if in preparation for some fairy house-keeping; there were jolly, broad-faced little men, much more agreeable in appearance than many real men—and no wonder, for their heads took off, and showed them to be full of sugar-plums; there were fiddles and drums; there were tambourines, books, work-boxes, paint-boxes, sweetmeat-boxes, peep-show boxes, and all kinds of boxes; there were trinkets for the elder girls, far brighter than any grown-up gold and jewels; there were baskets and pincushions in all devices; there were guns, swords, and banners; there were witches standing in enchanted rings of pasteboard, to tell fortunes; there were teeto-tums, humming-tops, needle-cases, pen-wipers, smelling-bottles, conversation-cards, boquet-holders, real fruit, made artificially dazzling with gold leaf; imitation apples, pears, and walnuts, crammed with surprises; in short, as a pretty child, before me, delightedly whispered to another pretty child, her bosom friend, "There was everything, and more." This motley collection of odd objects, clustering on the tree like magic fruit, and flashing back the bright looks directed towards it from every side—some of the dia-mond-eyes admiring it were hardly on a level with the table, and a few were languishing in timid wonder on the bosoms of pretty mothers, aunts, and nurses—made a lively realization of the fan-cies of childhood; and set me thinking how all the trees that grow, and all the things that come into existence on the earth, have their wild adornments at that well-remembered time.

Being now at home again, and alone, the only person in the house awake, my thoughts are drawn back, by a fascination which I do not care to resist, to my own childhood. I begin to consider, what do we all remember best upon the branches of the Christmas Tree of our own young Christmas days, by which we climbed to real life.

Straight, in the middle of the room, cramped in the freedom of its growth by no encircling walls or soon-reached ceiling, a shad-owy tree arises; and, looking up into the dreamy brightness of its top—for I observe in this tree the singular property that it appears to grow downward towards the earth—I look into my youngest Christmas recollections!

All toys at first, I find. Up yonder, among the green holly and red berries, is the Tumbler with his hands in his pockets, who wouldn't lie down, but whenever he was put upon the floor, persisted in rolling his fat body about, until he rolled himself still, and brought those lobster eyes of his to bear upon me—when I affected to laugh very much, but in my heart of hearts was extremely doubtful of him. Close beside him is that infernal snuff-box, out of which there sprang a demoniacal Counsellor in a black gown, with an obnoxious head of hair, and a red cloth mouth, wide open, who was not to be endured on any terms, but could not be put away either; for he used suddenly, in a highly magnified state, to fly out of Mammoth Snuff-boxes in dreams, when least expected. Nor is the frog with cobbler's wax on his tail, far off; for there was no knowing where he wouldn't jump; and when he flew over the candle, and came upon one's hand with that spotted back—red on a green ground—he was horrible. The cardboard lady in a blue-silk shirt, who was stood up against the candlestick to dance, and whom I see on the same branch, was milder, and was beautiful; but I can't say as much for the larger cardboard man, who used to be hung against the wall and pulled by a string; there was a sinister expression in that nose of his; and when he got his legs round his neck (which he very often did), he was ghastly, and not a creature to be alone with.

When did that dreadful Mask first look at me? Who put it on, and why was I so frightened that the sight of it is an era in my life? It is not a hideous visage in itself; it is even meant to be droll; why then were its stolid features so intolerable? Surely not because it hid the wearer's face. An apron would have done as much; and though I should have preferred even the apron away, it would not have been absolutely insupportable, like the mask. Was it the immovability of the mask? The doll's face was immovable, but I was not afraid of *her*. Perhaps that fixed and set change coming over a real face, infused into my quickened heart some remote suggestion and dread of the universal change that is to come on every face, and make it still? Nothing reconciled me to it. No drummers, from whom proceeded a melancholy chirping on the turning of a handle; no regiment of soldiers, with a mute band, taken out of a box, and fitted, one by one, upon a stiff and lazy little set of lazy-tongs;

no old woman, made of wires and brown-paper composition, cutting up a pie for two small children; could give me a permanent comfort, for a long time. Nor was it any satisfaction to be shown the Mask, and see that it was made of paper, or to have it locked up and be assured that no one wore it. The mere recollection of that fixed face, the mere knowledge of its existence anywhere, was sufficient to awake me in the night all perspiration and horror, with, "O I know it's coming! O the mask!"

I never wondered what the dear old donkey with the panniers—there he is!—was made of, then! His hide was real to the touch, I recollect. And the great black horse with the round red spots all over him—the horse that I could even get upon—I never wondered what had brought him to that strange condition, or thought that such a horse was not commonly seen at Newmarket. The four horses of no color, next to him, that went into the wagon of cheeses, and could be taken out and stabled under the piano, appear to have bits of fur-tippet for their tails, and other bits for their manes, and to stand on pegs instead of legs, but it was not so when they were brought home for a Christmas present. They were all right, then; neither was their harness unceremoniously nailed into their chests, as appears to be the case now. The tinkling works of the music-cart, I *did* find out, to be made of quill tooth-picks and wire; and I always thought that little tumbler in his shirt-sleeves, perpetually swarming up one side of wooden frame, and coming down, head foremost, on the other, rather a weak-minded person—though good-natured; but the Jacob's Ladder, next him, made of little squares of red wood, that went flapping and clattering over one another, each developing a different picture, and the whole enlivened by small bells, was a mighty marvel and a great delight.

Ah! The Doll's house!—of which I was not proprietor, but where I visited. I don't admire the Houses of Parliament half so much as that stone-fronted mansion with real glass windows, and door-steps, and a real balcony—greener than I ever see now, except at watering-places; and even they afford but a poor imitation. And though it *did* open all at once, the entire house-front (which was a blow, I admit, as cancelling the fiction of a staircase), it was but to shut it up again, and I could believe. Even open, there were three distinct rooms in it; a sitting-room and bed-room, elegantly furnished, and best of all, a kitchen, with uncommonly soft fire-irons, a plentiful assortment of diminutive utensils—oh, the warming-pan!—and a tin man-cook in profile, who was always going to fry two fish. What Barmecide justice have I done to the noble feasts wherein the set of wooden platters figured, each with its own peculiar delicacy, as a ham or turkey, glued tight on to it, and garnished with something green, which I recollect as moss! Could all the Temperance Societies of these latter days, united, give me such a tea-drinking as I have had through the means of yonder little set of blue crockery, which really would hold liquid (it ran out of the small wooden cask, I recollect, and tasted of matches), and which made tea, nectar. And if the two legs of the ineffectual little sugar-tongs did tumble over one another, and want purpose, like Punch's hands, what does it matter? And if I did once shriek out, as a poisoned child, and strike the fashionable company with consternation, by reason of having drunk a little teaspoon, inadvertently dissolved in too hot tea, I was never the worse for it, except by a powder!

Upon the next branches of the tree, lower down, hard by the green roller and miniature gardening-tools, how thick the goods begin to hang. Thin books, in themselves, at first, but many of them, and with deliciously smooth covers of bright red or green. What fat black letters to begin with! "A was an archer, and shot at a frog." Of course he was. He was an apple-pie also, and there he is! He was a good many things in his time, was A, and so were most of his friends, except X, who had so little versatility, that I never knew him to get beyond Xerxes or Xantippe—like Y, who was always confined to a Yacht or a Yew Tree; and Z condemned for ever to be a Zebra or a Zany. But, now, the very tree itself changes, and becomes a bean-stalk—the marvellous bean-stalk up which Jack climbed to the Giant's house! And now, those dreadfully interesting, double-headed giants, with their clubs over their shoulders, begin to stride along the boughs in a perfect throng, dragging knights and ladies home for dinner by the hair of their heads. And Jack—how noble, with his sword of sharpness, and his shoes of swiftness! Again those meditations come upon me as I gaze up at him; and I debate within myself whether there was more than one Jack (which I am loth to believe possible), or only one genuine original admirable Jack, who achieved all the record exploits.

Good for Christmas time is the ruddy color of the cloak, in which—the tree making a forest of itself for her to trip through, with her basket—Little Red Riding-Hood comes to me one Christmas Eve to give me information of the cruelty and treachery of that dissembling Wolf who ate her grandmother, without making any impression on his appetite, and then ate her, after making that ferocious joke about his teeth. She was my first love. I felt that if I could have married Little Red Riding-Hood, I should have known perfect bliss. But, it was not to be; and there was nothing for it but to look out the Wolf in the Noah's Ark there, and put him late in the procession on the table, as a monster who was to be degraded. O the wonderful Noah's Ark! It was not found seaworthy when put in a washing-tub, and the animals were crammed in at the roof, and needed to have their legs well shaken down before they could be got in, even there—and then, ten to one but they began to tumble out at the door, which was but imperfectly fastened with a wire latch—but what was *that* against it! Consider the noble fly, a size or two smaller than the elephant: the lady-bird, the butterfly—all triumphs of art! Consider the goose, whose feet were so small, and whose balance was so indifferent, that he usually tumbled forward, and knocked down all the animal creation. Consider Noah and his family, like idiotic tobacco stoppers; and how the leopard stuck to warm little fingers; and how the tails of the larger animals used gradually to resolve themselves into frayed bits of string!

Hush! Again a forest, and somebody up in a tree—not Robin Hood, not Valentine, not the Yellow Dwarf (I have passed him and all Mother Bunch's wonders, without mention), but an Eastern

King with a glittering scimitar and turban. By Allah! two Eastern Kings, for I see another, looking over his shoulder! Down upon the grass, at the tree's foot, lies the full length of a coal black Giant, stretched asleep, with his head in a lady's lap; and near them is a glass box, fastened with four blocks of shining steel, in which he keeps the lady prisoner when he is awake. I see the four keys at his girdle now. The lady makes signs to the two kings in the tree, who softly descend. It is the setting-in of the bright Arabian Nights.

Oh, now all common things become uncommon and enchanted to me. All lamps are wonderful; all rings are talismans. Common flower-pots are full of treasure, with a little earth scattered on the top; trees are for Ali Baba to hide in; beef-steaks are to throw down into the Valley of Diamonds, that the precious stones may stick to them, and be carried by the eagles to their nests, whence the traders, with loud cries, will scare them. Tarts are made, according to the recipe of the Vizier's son of Bussorah, who turned pastry-cook after he was set down in his drawers at the gate of Damascus; cobblers are all Mustaphas, and in the habit of sewing up people cut into four pieces, to whom they are taken blindfold.

Any iron ring let into stone is the entrance to a cave which only waits for the magician, and the little fire, and the necromancy, that will make the earth shake. All the dates imported come from the same tree as that unlucky date, with whose shell the merchant knocked out the eye of the genie's invisible son. All olives are of the stock of that fresh fruit, concerning which the Commander of the Faithful overheard the boy conduct the fictitious trial of the fraudulent olive merchant; all apples are akin to the apple purchased (with two others) from the Sultan's gardener for three sequins, and which the tall black slave stole from the child. All dogs are associated with the dog, really a transformed man, who jumped upon the baker's counter, and put his paw on the bad piece of money. All rice recalls the rice which the awful lady, who was a ghoule, could only peck by grains, because of her nightly feasts in the burial-place. My very rocking-horse,—there he is, with his nostrils turned completely inside-out, indicative of Blood!—should have a peg in his neck, by virtue thereof to fly away with me, as the wooden horse did with the Prince of Persia, in the sight of all his father's Court.

Yes, on every object that I recognize among those upper branches of my Christmas Tree, I see this fairy light! When I wake in bed, at daybreak, on the cold dark winter mornings, the white snow dimly beheld, outside, through the frost on the window pane, I hear Dinarzade. "Sister, sister, if you are yet awake, I pray you finish the history of the Young King of the Black Islands." Scheherazade replies, "If my lord the Sultan will suffer me to live another day, sister, I will not only finish that, but tell you a more wonderful story yet." Then, the gracious Sultan goes out, giving no orders for the execution, and we all three breathe again.

What images do I associate with the Christmas music as I see them set forth on the Christmas Tree? Known before all the others, keeping far apart from all the others, they gather round my little bed. An angel, speaking to a group of shepherds in a field; some travellers, with eyes uplifted, following a star; a baby in a manger; a child in a spacious temple, talking with grave men; a solemn figure, with a mild and beautiful face, raising a dead girl by the hand; again, near a city gate, calling back the son of a widow, on his bier, to life; a crowd of people looking through the opened roof of a chamber where he sits, and letting down a sick person on a bed, with ropes; the same, in a tempest, walking on the water to a ship; again, on a sea-shore, teaching a great multitude; again, with a child upon his knee, and other children round; again, restoring sight to the blind, speech to the dumb, hearing to the deaf, health to the sick, strength to the lame, knowledge to the ignorant; again, dying upon a Cross, watched by armed soldiers, a thick darkness coming on, the earth beginning to shake, and only one voice heard, "Forgive them, for they know not what they do."

Still, on the lower and maturer branches of the Tree, Christmas associations cluster thick. School-books shut up; Ovid and Virgil silenced; the Rule of Three, with its cool impertinent inquiries, long disposed of; Terence and Plautus acted no more, in an arena of huddled desks and forms, all chipped, and notched, and inked;

cricket-bats, stumps, and balls, left higher up, with the smell of trodden grass and the softened noise of shouts in the evening air; the tree is still fresh, still gay. If I no more come home at Christmas time, there will be boys and girls (thank Heaven!) while the World lasts; and they do! Yonder they dance and play upon the branches of my Tree, God bless them, merrily, and my heart dances and plays too!

And I *do* come home at Christmas. We all do, or we all should. We all come home, or ought to come home, for a short holiday—the longer, the better—from the great boarding-school, where we are for ever working at our arithmetical slates, to take, and give a rest. As to going a visiting, where can we not go, if we will; where have we not been, when we would; starting our fancy from our Christmas Tree!

Among the later toys and fancies hanging there—as idle often and less pure—be the images once associated with the sweet old Waits, the softened music in the night, ever unalterable! Encircled by the social thoughts of Christmas time, still let the benignant figure of my childhood stand unchanged! In every cheerful image and suggestion that the season brings, may the bright star that rested above the poor roof, be the star of all the Christian World! A moment's pause, O vanishing tree, of which the lower boughs are dark to me as yet, and let me look once more! I know there are blank spaces on thy branches, where eyes that I have loved, have shone and smiled; from which they are departed. But, far above, I see the raiser of the dead girl, and the Widow's Son; and God is good! If Age be hiding for me in the unseen portion of thy downward growth, O may I, with a gray head, turn a child's heart to that figure yet, and a child's trustfulness and confidence!

Now, the tree is decorated with bright merriment, and song, and dance, and cheerfulness. And they are welcome. Innocent and welcome be they ever held, beneath the branches of the Christmas Tree, which cast no gloomy shadow! But, as it sinks into the ground, I hear a whisper going through the leaves. "This, in commemoration of the law of love and kindness, mercy and compassion. This, in remembrance of Me!"

What
Christmas Is
As
We Grow Older

Therefore, as we grow older, let us be more thankful that the circle of our Christmas associations and of the lessons that they bring expands! Let us welcome every one of them, and summon them to take their places by the Christmas hearth.

Time was, with most of us, when Christmas Day encircling all our limited world like a magic ring, left nothing out for us to miss or seek; bound together all our home enjoyments, affections, and hopes; grouped everything and every one around the Christmas fire; and made the little picture shining in our bright young eyes, complete.

Time came, perhaps, all too soon, when our thoughts overleaped that narrow boundary; when there was some one (very dear, we thought then, very beautiful, and absolutely perfect) wanting to the fulness of our happiness; when we were wanting too (or we thought so, which did just as well) at the Christmas hearth by which that some one sat; and when we intertwined with every wreath and garland of our life that some one's name.

That was the time for the bright visionary Christmases which have long arisen from us to show faintly, after summer rain, in the palest edges of the rainbow! That was the time for the beatified enjoyment of the things that were to be, and never were, and yet the things that were so real in our resolute hope that it would be hard to say, now, what realities achieved since, have been stronger!

What! Did that Christmas never really come when we and the priceless pearl who was our young choice were received, after the happiest of totally impossible marriages, by the two united families previously at daggers-drawn on our account? When brothers and sisters in law who had always been rather cool to us before our relationship was effected, perfectly doted on us, and when fathers and mothers overwhelmed us with unlimited incomes? Was that Christmas dinner never really eaten, after which we arose, and generously and eloquently rendered honour to our late rival, present in the company, then and there exchanging friendship and forgiveness, and founding an attachment, not to be surpassed in Greek or Roman story, which subsisted until death? Has that same rival long ceased to care for that same priceless pearl, and married for money, and become usurious? Above all, do we really know, now, that we should probably have been miserable if we had won and worn the pearl, and that we are better without her?

That Christmas when we had recently achieved so much fame; when we had been carried in triumph somewhere, for doing something great and good; when we had won an honored and ennobled name, and arrived and were received at home in a shower of tears of joy; is it possible that *that* Christmas has not come yet?

And is our life here, at the best, so constituted that, pausing as we advance at such a noticeable milestone in the track as this great birthday, we look back on the things that never were, as naturally and full as gravely as on the things that have been and are gone, or have been and still are? If it be so, and so it seems to be, must we come to the conclusion that life is little better than a dream, and little worth the loves and strivings that we crowd into it?

No! Far be such miscalled philosophy from us, dear Reader, on Christmas Day! Nearer and closer to our hearts be the Christmas spirit, which is the spirit of active usefulness, perseverance, cheerful discharge of duty, kindness and forbearance! It is in the last virtues especially, that we are, or should be, strengthened by the unaccomplished visions of our youth; for, who shall say that they are not our teachers to deal gently even with the impalpable nothings of the earth!

Therefore, as we grow older, let us be more thankful that the circle of our Christmas associations and of the lessons that they bring expands! Let us welcome every one of them, and summon them to take their places by the Christmas hearth.

Welcome, old aspirations, glittering creatures of an ardent fancy, to your shelter underneath the holly! We know you, and have not outlived you yet. Welcome, old projects and old loves, however fleeting, to your nooks among the steadier lights that burn around us. Welcome, all that was ever real to our hearts; and for the earnestness that made you real, thanks to Heaven! Do we build no Christmas castles in the clouds now? Let our thoughts, fluttering like butterflies among these flowers of children, bear witness! Before this boy, there stretches out a Future, brighter than we ever looked on in our old romantic time, but bright with honour and with truth. Around this little head on which the sunny curls lie heaped, the graces sport, as prettily, as airily, as when there was no scythe within the reach of Time to shear away the curls of our first-love. Upon another girl's face near it—placider but smiling bright—a quiet and contented little face, we see Home fairly written. Shining from the word, as rays shine from a star, we see how, when our graves are old, other hopes than ours are young, other hearts than ours are moved; how other ways are smoothed; how other happiness blooms, ripens, and decays—no, not decays, for other homes and other bands of children, not yet in being nor for ages yet to be, arise, and bloom and ripen to the end of all!

Welcome, everything! Welcome, alike what has been, and what never was, and what we hope may be, to your shelter underneath the holly, to your places round the Christmas fire, where what is sits open-hearted! In yonder shadow, do we see obtruding furtively upon the blaze, an enemy's face? By Christmas Day we do forgive him! If the injury he has done us may admit of such companionship, let him come here and take his place. If otherwise, unhappily, let him go hence, assured that we will never injure nor accuse him.

On this day we shut out Nothing!

"Pause," says a low voice. "Nothing? Think!"

"On Christmas Day, we will shut out from our fireside, Nothing."

"Not the shadow of a vast City where the withered leaves are lying deep?" the voice replies. "Not the shadow that darkens the whole globe? Not the shadow of the City of the Dead?"

Not even that. Of all days in the year, we will turn our faces towards that City upon Christmas Day, and from its silent hosts bring those we loved, among us. City of the Dead, in the blessed name wherein we are gathered together at this time, and in the Presence that is here among us according to the promise, we will receive, and not dismiss, the people who are dear to us!

Yes. We can look upon these children angels that alight, so solemnly, so beautifully among the living children by the fire, and can bear to think how they departed from us. Entertaining angels unawares, as the Patriarchs did, the playful children are unconscious of their guests; but we can see them—can see a radiant arm around one favourite neck, as if there were a tempting of that child away. Among the celestial figures there is one, a poor mis-shapen boy on earth, of a glorious beauty now, of whom his dying mother said it grieved her much to leave him here, alone, for so many years as it was likely would elapse before he came to her—being such a little child. But he went quickly, and was laid upon her breast, and in her hand she leads him.

There was a gallant boy, who fell, far away, upon a burning sand beneath a burning sun, and said, "Tell them at home, with my last love, how much I could have wished to kiss them once, but that I died contented and had done my duty!" Or there was another, over whom they read the words, "Therefore we commit his body to the deep," and so consigned him to the lonely ocean and sailed on. Or there was another, who lay down to his rest in the dark shadow of great forests, and, on earth, awoke no more. O shall they not, from sand and sea and forest, be brought home at such a time?

There was a dear girl—almost a woman—never to be one—who made a mourning Christmas in a house of joy, and went her trackless way to the silent City. Do we recollect her, worn out, faintly whispering what could not be heard, and falling into that last deep sleep for weariness? O look upon her now! O look upon her beauty, her serenity, her changeless youth, her happiness! The daughter of Jairus was recalled to life, to die; but she, more blest, has heard the same voice, saying unto her, "Arise for ever!"

We had a friend who was our friend from early days, with whom we often pictured the changes that were to come upon our lives, and merrily imagined how we would speak, and walk, and think, and talk, when we came to be old. His destined habitation in the City of Dead received him in his prime. Shall he be shut out from our Christmas remembrance? Would his love have so excluded us? Lost friend, lost child, lost parent, sister, brother, husband, wife, we will not so discard you! You shall hold your cherished places in our Christmas hearts, and by our Christmas fires; and in the season of immortal hope, and on the birthday of immortal mercy, we will shut out Nothing!

The winter sun goes down over town and village; on the sea it makes a rosy path, as if the Sacred tread were fresh upon the water. A few more moments, and it sinks, and night comes on, and lights begin to sparkle in the prospect. On the hill-side beyond the shapelessly-diffused town, and in the quiet keeping of the trees that gird the village-steeple, remembrances are cut in stone, planted in common flowers, growing in grass, entwined with lowly brambles around many a mound of earth. In town and village, there are doors and windows closed against the weather, there are flaming logs heaped high, there are joyful faces, there is healthy music of voices. Be all ungentleness and harm excluded from the temples of the Household Gods, but be those remembrances admitted with tender encouragement! They are of the time and all its comforting and peaceful reassurances; and of the history that re-united even upon earth the living and the dead; and of the broad beneficence and goodness that too many men have tried to tear to narrow shreds.

A Walk in a Workhouse

Warm humanity pervades the Dickens Christmas, in it the paramount needs are those of the Child; he had always with him the Poor, whose poverty was not God's divine example, but man's crying shame. And he cried it, how he cried it, from the housetops!—Eleanor Farjeon, from Christmas Books *in The Oxford Illustrated Dickens series*

On a certain Sunday, I formed one of the congregation assembled in the chapel of a large metropolitan Workhouse. With the exception of the clergyman and clerk, and a very few officials, there were none but paupers present. The children sat in the galleries; the women in the body of the chapel, and in one of the side aisles; the men in the remaining aisle. The service was decorously performed, though the sermon might have been much better adapted to the comprehension and to the circumstances of the hearers. The usual supplications were offered, with more than the usual significancy in such a place, for the fatherless children and widows, for all sick persons and young children, for all that were desolate and oppressed, for the comforting and helping of the weak-hearted, for the raising-up of them that had fallen; for all that were in danger, necessity and tribulation. The prayers of the congregation were desired "for several persons in the various wards dangerously ill;" and others who were recovering returned their thanks to Heaven.

Among this congregation, were some evil-looking young women, and beetle-browed young men; but not many—perhaps that kind of characters kept away. Generally, the faces (those of the children excepted) were depressed and subdued, and wanted color. Aged people were there, in every variety. Mumbling, blear-eyed, spectacled, stupid, deaf, lame; vacantly winking in the gleams of sun that now and then crept in through the open doors, from the paved yard; shading their listening ears, or blinking eyes, with their withered hands; poring over their books, leering at nothing, going to sleep, crouching and drooping in corners. There were weird old women, all skeleton within, all bonnet and cloak without, continually wiping their eyes with dirty dusters of pocket handkerchiefs; and there were ugly old crones, both male and female, with a ghastly kind of contentment upon them which was not at all comforting to see. Upon the whole, it was the dragon, Pauperism, in a very weak and impotent condition; toothless, fangless, drawing his breath heavily enough, and hardly worth chaining up.

When the service was over I walked with the humane and conscientious gentleman whose duty it was to take that walk, that Sunday morning, through the little world of poverty enclosed within the workhouse walls. It was inhabited by a population of some fifteen hundred or two thousand paupers, ranging from the infant newly born or not yet come into the pauper world, to the old man dying on his bed.

In a room opening from a squalid yard, where a number of listless women were lounging to and fro, trying to get warm in the ineffectual sunshine of the tardy May morning—in the "Itch Ward," not to compromise the truth—a woman such as HOGARTH has often drawn, was hurriedly getting on her gown before a dusty fire. She was the nurse, or wardswoman, of that insalubrious department—herself a pauper—flabby, raw-boned, untidy—unpromising and coarse of aspect as need be. But, on being spoken to about the patients whom she had in charge, she turned round, with her shabby gown half on, half off, and fell a crying with all her might. Not for show, not querulously, not in any mawkish sentiment, but in the deep grief and affliction of her heart; turning away her dishevelled head: sobbing most bitterly, wringing her hands, and letting fall abundance of great tears that choked her utterance. What was the matter with the nurse of the Itch Ward? Oh, "the dropped child" was dead! Oh, the child that was found in the street, and she had brought up ever since, had died an hour ago, and see where the little creature lay, beneath this cloth! The dear, the pretty dear!

The dropped child seemed too small and poor a thing for Death to be in earnest with, but Death had taken it; and already its diminutive form was neatly washed, composed, and stretched as if in sleep upon a box. I thought I heard a voice from Heaven saying, It shall be well for thee, O nurse of the Itch Ward, when some less gentle pauper does those offices to thy cold form, that such as the dropped child are the angels who behold my Father's face!

In another room, were several ugly old women crouching, witch-like, round a hearth, and chattering and nodding, after the manner of the monkeys. "All well here? And enough to eat?" A general chattering and chuckling; at last an answer from a volunteer. "Oh yes, gentleman! Bless you gentleman! Lord bless the Parish of St. So-and-So! It feed the hungry, sir, and give drink to the thusty, and it warm them which is cold, so it do, and good luck to the parish of St. So-and-So, and thankee gentleman!" Elsewhere, a party of pauper nurses were at dinner. "How do *you* get on?" "Oh pretty well, sir! We works hard, and we lives hard—like the sodgers!"

In another room, a kind of purgatory or place of transition, six or eight noisy madwomen were gathered together, under the superintendence of one sane attendant. Among them was a girl of two or three-and-twenty, very prettily dressed, of most respectable appearance, and good manners, who had been brought in from the house where she had lived as domestic servant (having, I suppose, no friends), on account of being subject to epileptic fits, and requiring to be removed under the influence of a very bad one. She was by no means of the same stuff, or the same breeding, or the same experience, or in the same state of mind, as those by whom she was surrounded; and she pathetically complained that the daily association and the nightly noise made her worse, and was driving her mad—which was perfectly evident. The case was noted for inquiry and redress, but she said she had already been there for some weeks.

If this girl had stolen her mistress's watch, I do not hesitate to say she would have been infinitely better off. We have come to this absurd, this dangerous, this monstrous pass, that the dishonest felon is, in respect of cleanliness, order, diet, and accommodation, better provided for, and taken care of, than the honest pauper.

And this conveys no special imputation on the workhouse of the parish of St. So-and-So, where, on the contrary, I saw many things to commend. It was very agreeable, recollecting that most infamous and atrocious enormity committed at Tooting—an enormity which, a hundred years hence, will still be vividly remembered in the by-ways of English life, and which has done more to engender a gloomy discontent and suspicion among many thousands of the people than all the Chartist leaders could have done in all their lives—to find the pauper children in this workhouse looking robust and well, and apparently the objects of very great care. In the Infant School—a large, light, airy room at the top of the building— the little creatures, being at dinner, and eating their potatoes heartily, were not cowed by the presence of strange visitors, but stretched out their small hands to be shaken, with a very pleasant confidence. And it was comfortable to see two mangey pauper rocking-horses rampant in a corner. In the girls' school, where the dinner was also in process, everything bore a cheerful and healthy aspect. The meal was over, in the boys' school, by the time of our arrival there, and the room was not yet quite re-arranged; but the boys were roaming unrestrained about a large and airy yard, as any other schoolboys might have done. Some of them had been drawing large ships upon the school-room wall; and if they had a mast with shrouds and stays set up for practice (as they have in the Middlesex House of Correction), it would be so much the better. At present, if a boy should feel a strong impulse upon him to learn the art of going aloft, he could only gratify it, I presume, as the men and women paupers gratify their aspirations after better board and lodging, by smashing as many workhouse windows as possible, and being promoted to prison.

In one place, the Newgate of the Workhouse, a company of boys and youths were locked up in a yard alone; their day-room being a kind of kennel where the casual poor used formerly to be littered down at night. Divers of them had been there some long time. "Are they never going away?" was the natural inquiry. "Most of them are crippled, in some form or other," said the Wardsman, "and not fit for anything." They slunk about, like dispirited wolves or hyaenas; and made a pounce at their food when it was served out, much as those animals do. The big-headed idiot shuffling his feet along the pavement, in the sunlight outside, was a more agreeable object every way.

Groves of babies in arms; groves of mothers and other sick women in bed; groves of lunatics; jungles of men in stone-paved down stairs day-rooms, waiting for their dinners; longer and longer groves of old people, in up stairs Infirmary wards, wearing out life, God knows how—this was the scenery through which the walk lay, for two hours. In some of these latter chambers, there were pictures stuck against the wall, and a neat display of crockery and pewter on a kind of side-board; now and then it was a treat to see a plant or two; in almost every ward there was a cat.

In all of these Long Walks of aged and infirm, some old people were bedridden, and had been for a long time; some were sitting on their beds half-naked; some dying in their beds; some out of bed, and sitting at a table near the fire. A sullen or lethargic indifference to what was asked, a blunted sensibility to every-thing but warmth and food, a moody absence of complaint as being of no use, a dogged silence and resentful desire to be left alone again, I thought were generally apparent. On our walking into the midst of one of these dreary perspectives of old men, nearly the following little dialogue took place, the nurse not being immediately at hand:

"All well here?"

No answer. An old man in a Scotch cap sitting among others on a form at the table, eating out of a tin porringer, pushes back his cap a little to look at us, claps it down on his forehead again with the palm of his hand, and goes on eating.

"All well here?" (repeated.)

No answer. Another old man sitting on his bed, paralytically peeling a boiled potato, lifts his head and stares.

"Enough to eat?"

No answer. Another old man, in bed, turns himself and coughs.

"How are *you* to-day?" To the last old man.

That old man says nothing; but another old man, a tall old man of very good address, speaking with perfect correctness, comes forward from somewhere, and volunteers an answer. The reply almost always proceeds from a volunteer, and not from the person looked at or spoken to.

"We are very old, sir" in a mild, distinct voice. "We can't expect to be well, most of us."

"Are you comfortable?"

"I have no complaint to make, sir." With a half shake of his head, a half shrug of his shoulders, and a kind of apologetic smile.

"Enough to eat?"

"Why sir, I have but a poor appetite," with the same air as before; "and yet I get through my allowance very easily."

"But," showing a porringer with a Sunday dinner in it; "here is a portion of mutton, and three potatoes. You can't starve on that?"

"Oh dear no, sir," with the same apologetic air. "Not starve."

"What do you want?"

"We have very little bread, sir. It's an exceedingly small quantity of bread."

The nurse, who is now rubbing her hands at the questioner's elbow, interferes with, "It ain't much raly, sir. You see they've only six ounces a day, and when they've took their breakfast, there *can* only be a little left for night, sir."

Another old man, hitherto invisible, rises out of his bed-clothes, as out of a grave, and looks on.

"You have tea at night?" The questioner is still addressing the well-spoken old man.

"Yes, sir, we have tea at night."

"And you save what bread you can from the morning, to eat with it?"

"Yes, sir—if we can save any."

"And you want more to eat with it?"

"Yes, sir." With a very anxious face.

The questioner, in the kindness of his heart, appears a little discomposed, and changes the subject.

"What has become of the old man who used to lie in that bed in the corner?"

The nurse don't remember what old man is referred to. There has been such a many old men. The well-spoken old man is doubtful. The spectral old man who has come to life in bed, says, "Billy Stevens." Another old man who has previously had his head in the fire-place, pipes out,

"Charley Walters."

Something like a feeble interest is awakened. I suppose Charley Walters had conversation in him.

"He's dead," says the piping old man.

Another old man with one eye screwed up, hastily displaces the piping old man, and says:

"Yes! Charley Walters died in that bed, and—and—"

"Billy Stevens," persists the spectral old man.

"No, no! and Johnny Rogers died in that bed, and—and—they're both on 'em dead—and Sam'l Bowyer;" this seems very extraordinary to him; "he went out!"

With this he subsides, and all the old men (having had quite enough of it) subside, and the spectral old man goes into his grave again, and takes the shade of Billy Stevens with him.

As we turn to go out at the door, another previously invisible old man, a hoarse old man in a flannel gown, is standing there, as if he had just come up through the floor.

"I beg your pardon, sir, could I take the liberty of saying a word?"

"Yes; what is it?"

"I am greatly better in my health, sir; but what I want, to get me quite round," with his hand on his throat, "is a little fresh air, sir. It has always done my complaint so much good, sir. The regular leave for going out, comes round so seldom, that if the gentlemen, next Friday, would give me leave to go out walking, now and then—for only an hour or so, sir!—"

Who could wonder, looking through those weary vistas of bed and infirmity, that it should do him good to meet with some other scenes, and assure himself that there was something else on earth? Who could help wondering why the old men lived on as they did; what grasp they had on life; what crumbs of interest or occupation they could pick up from its bare board; whether Charley Walters had ever described to them the days when he kept company with some old pauper woman in the bud, or Billy Stevens ever told them of the time when he was a dweller in the far-off foreign land called Home!

The morsel of burnt child, lying in another room, so patiently, in bed, wrapped in lint, and looking steadfastly at us with his bright quiet eyes when we spoke to him kindly, looked as if the knowledge of these things, and of all the tender things there are to think about, might have been in his mind—as if he thought, with us, that there was a fellow-feeling in the pauper nurses which appeared to make them more kind to their charges than the race of common nurses in the hospitals—as if he mused upon the Future of some older children lying around him in the same place, and thought it best, perhaps, all things considered, that he should die—as if he knew, without fear, of those many coffins, made and unmade, piled up in the store below—and of his unknown friend, "the dropped child," calm upon the box-lid covered with a cloth. But there was

something wistful and appealing, too, in his tiny face, as if, in the
midst of all the hard necessities and incongruities he pondered on,
he pleaded in behalf of the helpless and the aged poor, for a little
more liberty—and a little more bread.

A Walk
in the
Winter Woods

Thus Christmas begirt me, far and near....

Going through the woods, the softness of my tread upon the mossy ground and among the brown leaves enhanced the Christmas sacredness by which I felt surrounded. As the whitened stems environed me, I thought how the Founder of the time had never raised his benignant hand, save to bless and heal, except in the case of one unconscious tree. By Cobham Hall, I came to the village, and the churchyard where the dead had been quietly buried, "in the sure and certain hope" which Christmas time inspired. What children could I see at play, and not be loving of, recalling who had loved them! No garden that I passed was out of unison with the day, for I remembered that the tomb was in a garden, and that "she, supposing him to be the gardener," had said, "Sir, if thou have borne him hence, tell me where thou hast laid him, and I will take him away." In time, the distant river with the ships came full in view, and with it pictures of the poor fishermen, mending their nets, who arose and followed him,—of the teaching of the people from a ship pushed off a little way from shore, by reason of the multitude,—of a majestic figure walking on the water, in the loneliness of night.

My very shadow on the ground was eloquent of Christmas; for did not the people lay their sick where the mere shadow of the men who had heard and seen him might fall as they passed along?

Thus Christmas begirt me, far and near, until I had come to Blackheath, and had walked down the long vista of gnarled old trees in Greenwich Park, and was being steam-rattled through the mists now closing in once more, towards the lights of London. Brightly they shone, but not so brightly as my own fire, and the brighter faces around it, when we came together to celebrate the day. And there I told of worthy Master Richard Watts, and of my supper with the Six Poor Travellers who were neither Rogues nor Proctors, and from that hour to this I have never seen one of them again.—*from "The Seven Poor Travellers"*

Great Expectations

(Chapter IV)

It began the moment we sat down to dinner. Mr. Wopsle said grace with theatrical declamation—as it now appears to me, something like a religious cross of the Ghost in Hamlet with Richard the Third—and ended with the very proper aspiration that we might be truly grateful. Upon which my sister fixed me with her eye, and said, in a low reproachful voice, "Do you hear that? Be grateful."

I fully expected to find a Constable in the kitchen, waiting to take me up. But not only was there no Constable there, but no discovery had yet been made of the robbery. Mrs. Joe was prodigiously busy in getting the house ready for the festivities of the day, and Joe had been put upon the kitchen door-step to keep him out of the dust-pan—an article into which his destiny always led him, sooner or later, when my sister was vigorously reaping the floors of her establishment.

"And where the deuce ha' *you* been?" was Mrs. Joe's Christmas salutation, when I and my conscience showed ourselves.

I said I had been down to hear the Carols. "Ah! well!" observed Mrs. Joe. "You might ha' done worse." Not a doubt of that, I thought.

"Perhaps if I warn't a blacksmith's wife, and (what's the same thing) a slave with her apron never off, *I* should have been to hear the Carols," said Mrs. Joe. "I'm rather partial to Carols myself, and that's the best of reasons for my never hearing any."

Joe, who had ventured into the kitchen after me as the dustpan had retired before us, drew the back of his hand across his nose with a conciliatory air, when Mrs. Joe darted a look at him, and, when her eyes were withdrawn, secretly crossed his two forefingers, and exhibited them to me, as our token that Mrs. Joe was in a cross temper. This was so much her normal state, that Joe and I would often, for weeks together, be, as to our fingers, like monumental Crusaders as to their legs.

We were to have a superb dinner, consisting of a leg of pickled pork and greens, and a pair of roast stuffed fowls. A handsome mince-pie had been made yesterday morning (which accounted for the mince-meat not being missed), and the pudding was already on the boil. These extensive arrangements occasioned us to be cut off unceremoniously in respect of breakfast; "for I ain't," said Mrs. Joe, "I ain't a-going to have no formal cramming and busting and washing up now, with what I've got before me, I promise you!"

So, we had our slices served out, as if we were two thousand troops on a forced march instead of a man and boy at home; and we took gulps of milk and water, with apologetic countenances, from a jug on the dresser. In the meantime, Mrs. Joe put clean white curtains up, and tacked a new flowered-flounce across the wide chimney to replace the old one, and uncovered the little state parlour across the passage, which was never uncovered at any other time, but passed the rest of the year in a cool haze of silver paper, which even extended to the four little white crockery poodles on the mantleshelf, each with a black nose, and a basket of flowers in his mouth, and each the counterpart of the other. Mrs. Joe was a very clean housekeeper, but had an exquisite art of making her cleanliness more uncomfortable and unacceptable than dirt itself. Cleanliness is next to Godliness, and some people do the same by their religion.

My sister having so much to do, was going to church vicariously; that is to say, Joe and I were going. In his working clothes,

Joe was a well-knit characteristic-looking blacksmith; in his holiday clothes, he was more like a scarecrow in good circumstances, than anything else. Nothing that he wore then, fitted him or seemed to belong to him; and everything that he wore then, grazed him. On the present festive occasion he emerged from his room, when the blithe bells were going, the picture of misery, in a full suit of Sunday penitentials. As to me, I think my sister must have had some general idea that I was a younger offender whom an Accoucheur Policeman had taken up (on my birthday) and delivered over to her, to be dealt with according to the outraged majesty of the law. I was always treated as if I had insisted on being born in opposition to the dictates of reason, religion, and morality, and against the dissuading arguments of my best friends. Even when I was taken to have a new suit of clothes, the tailor had orders to make them like a kind of Reformatory, and on no account to let me have the free use of my limbs.

Joe and I going to church, therefore, must have been a moving spectacle for compassionate minds. Yet, what I suffered outside, was nothing to what I underwent within. The terrors that had assailed me whenever Mrs. Joe had gone near the pantry, or out of the room, were only to be equalled by the remorse with which my mind dwelt on what my hands had done. Under the weight of my wicked secret, I pondered whether the Church would be powerful enough to shield me from the vengeance of the terrible young man, if I divulged to that establishment. I conceived the idea that the time when the banns were read and when the clergyman said, "Ye are now to declare it!" would be the time for me to rise and propose a private conference in the vestry. I am far from being sure that I might not have astonished our small congregation by resorting to this extreme measure, but for its being Christmas Day and no Sunday.

Mr. Wopsle, the clerk at church, was to dine with us; and Mr. Hubble, the wheelwright, and Mrs. Hubble; and Uncle Pumblechook (Joe's uncle, but Mrs. Joe appropriated him), who was a well-to-do cornchandler in the nearest town, and drove his own chaise-cart. The dinner hour was half-past one. When Joe and I got

home, we found the table laid, and Mrs. Joe dressed, and the dinner dressing, and the front door unlocked (it never was at any other
time) for the company to enter by, and everything most splendid.
And still, not a word of the robbery.

The time came, without bringing with it any relief to my feelings, and the company came. Mr. Wopsle, united to a Roman nose
and a large shining bald forehead, had a deep voice which he was
uncommonly proud of; indeed it was understood among his acquaintance that if you could only give him his head, he would read
the clergyman into fits; he himself confessed that if the Church was
"thrown open," meaning his mark in it. The Church not being
"thrown open," he was, as I have said, our clerk. But he punished
the Amens tremendously; and when he gave out the psalm—always giving the whole verse—he looked all around the congregation first, as much as to say, "You have heard our friend overhead;
oblige me with your opinion of this style!"

I opened the door to the company—making believe that it was a
habit of ours to open the door—and I opened it first to Mr. Wopsle,
next to Mr. and Mrs. Hubble, and last of all to Uncle Pumblechook.
N.B. *I* was not allowed to call him uncle, under the severest penalties.

"Mrs. Joe," said Uncle Pumblechook; a large hard-breathing,
middle-aged slow man, with a mouth like a fish, dull staring eyes,
and sandy hair standing upright on his head, so that he looked as if
he had just been all but choked, and had that moment come to; "I
have brought you as the compliments of the season—I have
brought you, Mum, a bottle of sherry wine—and I have brought
you, Mum, a bottle of port wine."

Every Christmas Day he presented himself, as a profound novelty, with exactly the same words, and carrying the two bottles like
dumb-bells. Every Christmas Day, Mrs. Joe replied, as she now
replied, "Oh, Un—cle Pum—ble—chook! This is kind!" Every
Christmas Day he retorted, as he now retorted, "It's no more than
your merits. And now are you all bobbish, and how's Sixpennorth
of halfpence?" meaning me.

We dined on these occasions in the kitchen, and adjourned, for the nuts and oranges and apples, to the parlour; which was a change very like Joe's change from his working clothes to his Sunday dress. My sister was uncommonly lively on the present occasion, and indeed was generally more gracious in the society of Mrs. Hubble than in other company. I remember Mrs. Hubble as a little curly sharp-edged person in sky-blue, who held a conventionally juvenile position, because she had married Mr. Hubble—I don't know at what remote period—when she was much younger than he. I remember Mr. Hubble as a tough high-shouldered stooping old man, of a sawdusty fragrance, with his legs extraordinarily wide apart: so that in my short days I always saw some miles of open country between them when I met him coming up the lane.

Among this good company I should have felt myself, even if I hadn't robbed the pantry, in a false position. Not because I was squeezed in at an acute angle of the table-cloth, with the table in my chest, and the Pumblechookian elbow in my eye, nor because I was not allowed to speak (I didn't want to speak), nor because I was regaled with the scaly tips of the drumsticks of the fowls, and with those obscure corners of pork of which the pig, when living, had had the least reason to be vain. No; I should not have minded that if they would only have left me alone. But they wouldn't leave me alone. They seemed to think the opportunity lost, if they failed to point the conversation at me, every now and then, and stick the point into me. I might have been an unfortunate little bull in a Spanish arena, I got so smartingly touched up by these moral goads.

It began the moment we sat down to dinner. Mr. Wopsle said grace with theatrical declamation—as it now appears to me, something like a religious cross of the Ghost in Hamlet with Richard the Third—and ended with the very proper aspiration that we might be truly grateful. Upon which my sister fixed me with her eye, and said, in a low reproachful voice, "Do you hear that? Be grateful."

"Especially," said Mr. Pumblechook, "be grateful, boy, to them which brought you up by hand."

Mrs. Hubble shook her head, and contemplating me with a mournful presentiment that I should come to no good, asked, "Why is it that the young are never grateful?" This moral mystery seemed too much for the company until Mr. Hubble tersely solved it by saying, "Naterally wicious." Everybody then murmured "True!" and looked at me in a particularly unpleasant and personal manner.

Joe's station and influence were something feebler (if possible) when there was company, than when there was none. But he always aided and comforted me when he could, in some way of his own, and he always did so at dinner-time by giving me gravy, if there were any. There being plenty of gravy to-day, Joe spooned into my plate, at this point, about half a pint.

A little later on in the dinner, Mr. Wopsle reviewed the sermon with some severity, and intimated—in the usual hypothetical case of the Church being "thrown open"—what kind of sermon *he* would have given them. After favouring them with some heads of that discourse, he remarked that he considered the subject of the day's homily, ill-chosen; which was the less excusable, he added, when there were so many subjects "going about."

"True again," said Uncle Pumblechook. "You've hit it, sir! Plenty of subjects going about, for them that know how to put salt upon their tails. That's what's wanted. A man needn't go far to find a subject, if he's ready with his salt-box." Mr. Pumblechook added, after a short interval of reflection, "Look at Pork alone. There's a subject! If you want a subject, look at Pork!"

"True, sir. Many a moral for the young," returned Mr. Wopsle; and I knew he was going to lug me in, before he said it, "might be deduced from that text."

("You listen to this," said my sister to me, in a severe parenthesis.)

Joe gave me some more gravy.

"Swine," pursued Mr. Wopsle, in his deepest voice, and pointing his fork at my blushes, as if he were mentioning my christian name, "Swine were the companions of the prodigal. The gluttony of

Swine is put before us, as an example to the young." (I thought this pretty well in him who had been praising up the pork for being so plump and juicy.) "What is detestable in a pig, is more detestable in a boy."

"Or girl," suggested Mr. Hubble.

"Of course, or girl, Mr. Hubble," assented Mr. Wopsle, rather irritably, "but there is no girl present."

"Besides," said Mr. Pumblechook, turning sharp on me, "think what you've got to be grateful for. If you'd been born a Squeaker——"

"He *was*, if ever a child was," said my sister, most emphatically.

Joe gave me some more gravy.

"Well, but I mean a four-footed Squeaker," said Mr. Pumblechook. "If you had been born such, would you have been here now? Not you——"

"Unless in that form," said Mr. Wopsle, nodding towards the dish.

"But I don't mean in that form, sir," returned Mr. Pumblechook, who had an objection to being interrupted; "I mean, enjoying himself with his elders and betters, and improving himself with their conversation, and rolling in the lap of luxury. Would he have been doing that? No, he wouldn't. And what would have been your destination?" turning on me again. "You would have been disposed of for so many shillings according to the market price of the article, and Dunstable the butcher would have come up to you as you lay in your straw, and he would have whipped you under his left arm, and with his right he would have tucked up his frock to get a penknife from out of his waistcoat-pocket, and he would have shed your blood and had your life. No bringing up by hand then. Not a bit of it!"

Joe offered me more gravy, which I was afraid to take.

"He was a world of trouble to you, ma'am," said Mrs. Hubble, commiserating my sister.

"Trouble?" echoed my sister, "trouble?" And then entered on a fearful catalogue of all the illnesses I had been guilty of, and all the acts of sleeplessness I had committed, and all the high places I had tumbled from, and all the low places I had tumbled into, and all the injuries I had done myself, and all the times she had wished me in my grave, and I had contumaciously refused to go there.

I think the Romans must have aggravated one another very much, with their noses. Perhaps they became the restless people they were, in consequence. Anyhow, Mr. Wopsle's Roman nose so aggravated me, during the recital of my misdemeanours, that I should have liked to pull it until he howled. But, all I had endured up to this time, was nothing in comparison with the awful feelings that took possession of me when the pause was broken which ensued upon my sister's recital, and in which pause everybody had looked at me (as I felt painfully conscious) with indignation and abhorrence.

"Yet," said Mr. Pumblechook, leading the company gently back to the theme from which they had strayed, "Pork—regarded as biled—is rich, too; ain't it?"

"Have a little brandy, uncle," said my sister.

O Heavens, it had come at last! He would find it was weak, he would say it was weak, and I was lost! I held tight to the leg of the table, under the cloth, with both hands, and awaited my fate.

My sister went for the stone bottle, came back with the stone bottle, and poured his brandy out: no one else taking any. The wretched man trifled with his glass—took it up, looked at it through the light, put it down—prolonged my misery. All this time Mrs. Joe and Joe were briskly clearing the table for the pie and pudding.

I couldn't keep my eyes off him. Always holding tight by the leg of the table with my hands and feet, I saw the miserable creature finger his glass playfully, take it up, smile, throw his head back, and drink the brandy off. Instantly afterwards, the company were seized with unspeakable consternation, owing to his springing to his feet, turning round several times in an appalling spasmodic whooping-cough dance, and rushing out at the door; he then became visible through the window, violently plunging and expectorating, making the most hideous faces, and apparently out of his mind.

I held on tight, while Mrs. Joe and Joe ran to him. I didn't know how I had done it, but I had no doubt I had murdered him somehow. In my dreadful situation, it was a relief when he was brought back, and, surveying the company all round as if *they* had disagreed with him, sank down into his chair with the one significant gasp, "Tar!"

I had filled up the bottle from the Tar-water jug. I knew he would be worse by-and-by. I moved the table, like a Medium of the present day, by the vigour of my unseen hold upon it.

"Tar!" said my sister, in amazement. "Why, how ever could Tar come there?"

But Uncle Pumblechook, who was omnipotent in that kitchen, wouldn't hear the word, wouldn't hear of the subject, imperiously waved it all away with his hand, and asked for hot gin-and-water. My sister, who had begun to be alarmingly meditative, had to employ herself actively in getting the gin, the hot water, the sugar, and the lemon peel, and mixing them. For the time at least, I was saved. I still held on to the leg of the table, but clutched it now with the fervour of gratitude.

By degrees, I became calm enough to release my grasp, and partake of pudding. Mr. Pumblechook partook of pudding. All partook of pudding. The course terminated, and Mr. Pumblechook had begun to beam under the genial influence of gin-and-water. I began to think I should get over the day, when my sister said to Joe, "Clean plates—cold."

I clutched the leg of the table again immediately, and pressed it to my bosom as if it had been the companion of my youth and friend of my soul. I foresaw what was coming, and I felt that this time I really was gone.

"You must taste," said my sister, addressing the guests with her best grace. "You must taste, to finish with, such a delightful and delicious present of Uncle Pumblechook's!"

Must they! Let them not hope to taste it!

"You must know," said my sister, rising, "it's a pie; a savoury pork pie."

The company murmured their compliments. Uncle Pumblechook, sensible of having deserved well of his fellow-creatures, said—quite vivaciously, all things considered—"Well, Mrs. Joe, we'll do our best endeavours; let us have a cut at this same pie."

My sister went out to get it. I heard her steps proceed to the pantry. I saw Mr. Pumblechook balance his knife. I saw re-awakening appetite in the Roman nostrils of Mr. Wopsle. I heard Mr. Hubble remark that "a bit of savoury pork pie would lay atop of anything you could mention, and do no harm," and I heard Joe say, "You shall have some, Pip." I never have been absolutely certain whether I uttered a shrill yell of terror, merely in spirit, or in the bodily hearing of the company. I felt that I could bear no more, and that I must run away. I released the leg of the table, and ran for my life.

But I ran no further than the house door, for there I ran head foremost into a party of soldiers with their muskets: one of whom held out a pair of handcuffs to me, saying, "Here you are, look sharp, come on!"

The Pickwick Papers

(excerpts from Chapters XXVIII and XXIX)

"This," said Mr. Pickwick, looking round him, "this is, indeed, comfort."

"Our invariable custom," replied Mr. Wardle. "Everybody sits down with us on Christmas eve, as you see them now—servants and all; and here we wait, until the clock strikes twelve, to usher Christmas in, and beguile the time with forfeits and old stories. Trundle, my boy, rake up the fire."

As brisk as bees, if not altogether as light as fairies, did the four Pickwickians assemble on the morning of the twenty-second day of December, in the year of grace in which these, their faithfully-recorded adventures, were undertaken and accomplished. Christmas was close at hand, in all his bluff and hearty honesty; it was the season of hospitality, merriment, and open-heartedness; the old year was preparing, like an ancient philosopher, to call his friends around him, and amidst the sound of feasting and revelry to pass gently and calmly away. Gay and merry was the time, and gay and merry were at least four of the numerous hearts that were gladdened by its coming.

And numerous indeed are the hearts to which Christmas brings a brief season of happiness and enjoyment. How many families, whose members have been dispersed and scattered far and wide, in the restless struggles of life, are then reunited, and meet once again in that happy state of companionship and mutual good-will, which is a source of such pure and un-alloyed delight, and one so incompatible with the cares and sorrows of the world, that the religious belief of the most civilised nations, and the rude traditions of the roughest savages, alike number it among the first joys of a future condition of existence, provided for the blest and happy! How many old recollections, and how many dormant sympathies, does Christmas time awaken!

We write these words now, many miles distant from the spot at which, year after year, we met on that day, a merry and joyous circle. Many of the hearts that throbbed so gaily then, have ceased to beat; many of the looks that shone so brightly then, have ceased to glow; the hands we grasped have grown cold; the eyes we sought have hid their lustre in the grave; and yet the old house, the room, the merry voices and smiling faces, the jest, the laugh, the most minute and trivial circumstances connected with those happy meetings, crowd upon our mind at each recurrence of the season, as if the last assemblage had been but yesterday! Happy, happy Christmas, that can win us back to the delusions of our childish days; that can recall to the old man the pleasures of his youth; that can transport the sailor and the traveller, thousands of miles away, back to his own fire-side and his quiet home!

A happy party they were, that night. Pickwick and the old lady played together; uproarious was the mirth of the round table. Long after the ladies had retired, did the hot elder wine, well qualified with brandy and spice, go round, and round, and round again; and sound was the sleep and pleasant were the dreams that followed. It is a remarkable fact that those of Mr. Snodgrass bore constant reference to Emily Wardle; and that the principal figure in Mr. Winkle's visions was a young lady with black eyes, an arch smile, and a pair of remarkably nice boots with fur round the tops.

Mr. Pickwick was awakened, early in the morning, by a hum of voices and a pattering of feet, sufficient to rouse even the fat boy from his heavy slumbers. He sat up in bed and listened. The female servants and female visitors were running constantly to and fro; and there were such multitudinous demands for hot water, such repeated outcries for needles and thread, and so many half-suppressed entreaties of 'Oh, do come and tie me, there's a dear!' that Mr. Pickwick in his innocence began to imagine that something dreadful must have occurred: when he grew more awake, and remembered the wedding. The occasion being an important one he dressed himself with peculiar care, and descended to the breakfast room.

There were all the female servants in a brand new uniform of pink muslin gowns with white bows in their caps, running about the house in a state of excitement and agitation which it would be impossible to describe. The old lady was dressed out in a brocaded gown which had not seen the light for twenty years, saving and excepting such truant rays as had stolen through the chinks in the box in which it had been lain by, during the whole time. Mr. Trundle was in high feather and spirits, but a little nervous withal. The hearty old landlord was trying to look very cheerful and unconcerned, but failing signally in the attempt. All the girls were in tears and white muslin, except a select two or three who were being honoured with a private view of the bride and bridesmaids, up stairs. All the Pickwickians were in most blooming array; and there was a terrific roaring on the grass in front of the house, occasioned by all the men, boys, and hobbledehoys attached to the farm, each of whom had got a white bow in his button-hole, and all of whom were cheering with might and main: being incited thereunto, and stimulated therein, by the precept and example of Mr. Samuel Weller, who had managed to become mighty popular already, and was as much at home as if he had been born on the land.

A wedding is a licensed subject to joke upon, but there really is no great joke in the matter after all;—we speak merely of the ceremony, and beg it to be distinctly understood that we indulge in no hidden sarcasm upon a married life. Mixed up with the pleasure and joy of the occasion, are the many regrets at quitting home, the tears of parting between parent and child, the consciousness of leaving the dearest and kindest friends of the happiest portion of human life, to encounter its cares and troubles with others still untried and little known: natural feelings which we would not render this chapter mournful by describing, and which we should be still more unwilling to be supposed to ridicule.

Let us briefly say, then, that the ceremony was performed by the old clergyman, in the parish church of Dingley Dell, and that Mr. Pickwick's name is attached to the register, still preserved in the vestry thereof; that the young lady with the black eyes signed her name in a very unsteady and tremulous manner; that Emily's signature, as the other bridesmaid, is nearly illegible; that it all went off in very admirable style; that the young ladies generally thought it far less shocking than they had expected; and that although the owner of the black eyes and the arch smile informed Mr. Winkle that she was sure she could never submit to anything so dreadful, we have the very best reasons for thinking she was mistaken. To all this, we may add, that Mr. Pickwick was the first who saluted the bride, and that in so doing, he threw over her neck a rich gold watch and chain, which no mortal eyes but the jeweller's had ever beheld before. Then, the old church bell rang as gaily as it could, and they all returned to breakfast.

'Vere does the mince pies go, young opium eater?' said Mr. Weller to the fat boy, as he assisted in laying out such articles of consumption as had not been duly arranged on the previous night.

The fat boy pointed to the destination of the pies.

'Wery good,' said Sam, 'stick a bit o' Christmas in 'em. T'other dish opposite. There; now we look compact and comfortable, as the father said ven he cut his little boy's head off, to cure him o' squintin'.'

As Mr. Weller made the comparison, he fell back a step or two, to give full effect to it, and surveyed the preparations with the utmost satisfaction.

'Wardle,' said Mr. Pickwick, almost as soon as they were all seated, 'a glass of wine, in honour of this happy occasion!'

'I shall be delighted, my boy,' said Mr. Wardle. 'Joe—damn that boy, he's gone to sleep.'

'No, I ain't, sir,' replied the fat boy, starting up from a remote corner, where, like the patron saint of fat boys—the immortal Horner—he had been devouring a Christmas pie: though not with the coolness and deliberation which characterised that young gentleman's proceedings.

'Fill Mr. Pickwick's glass.'

'Yes, sir.'

The fat boy filled Mr. Pickwick's glass, and then retired behind his master's chair, from whence he watched the play of the knives and forks, and the progress of the choice morsels from the dishes to the mouths of the company, with a kind of dark and gloomy joy that was most impressive.

'God bless you, old fellow!' said Mr. Pickwick.

'Same to you, my boy,' replied Wardle; and they pledged each other, heartily.

'Mrs. Wardle,' said Mr. Pickwick, 'we old folks must have a glass of wine together, in honour of this joyful event.'

The old lady was in a state of great grandeur just then, for she was sitting at the top of the table in the brocaded gown, with her newly-married grand-daughter on one side and Mr. Pickwick on the other, to do the carving. Mr. Pickwick had not spoken in a very loud tone, but she understood him at once, and drank off a full glass of wine to his long life and happiness; after which the worthy old soul launched forth into a minute and particular account of her own wedding, with a dissertation on the fashion of wearing high-heeled shoes, and some particulars concerning the life and adventures of the beautiful Lady Tollimglower, deceased: at all of which the old lady herself laughed very heartily indeed, and so did the young ladies too, for they were wondering among themselves what on earth grandma was talking about. When they laughed, the old lady laughed ten times more heartily, and said that these always had been considered capital stories: which caused them all to laugh again, and put the old lady into the very best of humours.

Then, the cake was cut, and passed through the ring; the young ladies saved pieces to put under their pillows to dream of their future husbands on; and a great deal of blushing and merriment was thereby occasioned.

'Mr. Miller,' said Mr. Pickwick to his old acquaintance the hard-headed gentleman, 'a glass of wine?'

'With great satisfaction, Mr. Pickwick,' replied the hard-headed gentleman, solemnly.

'You'll take me in?' said the benevolent old clergyman.

'And me,' interposed his wife.

'And me, and me,' said a couple of poor relations at the bottom of the table, who had eaten and drank very heartily, and laughed at everything.

Mr. Pickwick expressed his heartfelt delight at every additional suggestion; and his eyes beamed with hilarity and cheerfulness.

'Ladies and gentlemen,' said Mr. Pickwick, suddenly rising.

'Hear, hear! Hear, hear! Hear, hear!' cried Mr. Weller, in the excitement of his feelings.

'Call in all the servants,' cried old Wardle, interposing to prevent the public rebuke which Mr. Weller would otherwise most indubitably have received from his master. 'Give them a glass of wine each, to drink the toast in. Now, Pickwick.'

Amidst the silence of the company, the whispering of the women servants, and the awkward embarrassment of the men, Mr. Pickwick proceeded.

'Ladies and gentlemen—no, I won't say ladies and gentlemen, I'll call you my friends, my dear friends, if the ladies will allow me to take so great a liberty'——

Here Mr. Pickwick was interrupted by immense applause from the ladies, echoed by the gentlemen, during which the owner of the eyes was distinctly heard to state that she could kiss that dear Mr. Pickwick. Whereupon Mr. Winkle gallantly inquired if it couldn't be done by deputy: to which the young lady with the black eyes replied, 'Go away'—and accompanied the request with a look which said as plainly as a look could do——'if you can.'

'My dear friends,' resumed Mr. Pickwick, 'I am going to propose the health of the bride and bridegroom—God bless 'em (cheers and tears). My young friend, Trundle, I believe to be a very excellent and manly fellow; and his wife I know to be a very amiable and lovely girl, well qualified to transfer to another sphere of action the happiness which for twenty years she has diffused around her, in her father's house. (Here, the fat boy burst forth into stentorian blubberings, and was led forth by the coat collar, by Mr. Weller.) I wish,' added Mr. Pickwick, 'I wish I was young enough to be her sister's husband (cheers), but, failing that, I am happy to be old enough to be her father; for, being so, I shall not be suspected of any latent designs when I say, that I admire, esteem, and love them both (cheers and sobs). The bride's father, our good friend there, is a noble person, and I am proud to know him (great uproar). He is a kind, excellent, independent-spirited, fine-hearted, hospitable, liberal man (enthusiastic shouts from the poor relations, at all the adjectives; and especially at the two last). That his daughter may enjoy all the happiness, even he can desire; and that he may derive from the contemplation of her felicity all the gratification of heart and peace of mind which he so well deserves, is, I am persuaded, our united wish. So, let us drink their healths, and wish them prolonged life, and every blessing!'

Mr. Pickwick concluded amidst a whirlwind of applause; and once more were the lungs of the supernumeraries, under Mr. Weller's command, brought into active and efficient operation. Mr. Wardle proposed Mr. Pickwick; Mr. Pickwick proposed the old lady. Mr. Snodgrass proposed Mr. Wardle; Mr. Wardle proposed Mr. Snodgrass. One of the poor relations proposed Mr. Tupman, and the other poor relation proposed Mr. Winkle; all was happiness and festivity, until the mysterious disappearance of both the poor relations beneath the table, warned the party that it was time to adjourn.

At dinner they met again, after a five-and-twenty mile walk, undertaken by the males at Wardle's recommendation, to get rid of the effects of the wine at breakfast. The poor relations had kept in

bed all day, with the view of attaining the same happy consumma-
tion, but, as they had been unsuccessful, they stopped there. Mr.
Weller kept the domestics in a state of perpetual hilarity; and the fat
boy divided his time into small alternate allotments of eating and
sleeping.

The dinner was as hearty an affair as the breakfast, and was
quite as noisy, without the tears. Then came the dessert and some
more toasts. Then came the tea and coffee; and then, the ball.

The best sitting-room at Manor Farm was a good, long, dark-
panelled room with a high chimney-piece, and a capacious chimney, up which you could have driven one of the new patent cabs,
wheels and all. At the upper end of the room, seated in a shady
bower of holly and evergreens, were the two best fiddlers, and the
only harp, in all Muggleton. In all sorts of recesses, and on all kinds
of brackets, stood massive old silver candlesticks with four
branches each. The carpet was up, the candles burnt bright, the fire
blazed and crackled on the hearth, and merry voices and light-
hearted laughter rang through the room. If any of the old English
yeomen had turned into fairies when they died, it was just the
place in which they would have held their revels.

If anything could have added to the interest of this agreeable
scene, it would have been the remarkable fact of Mr. Pickwick's
appearing without his gaiters, for the first time within the memory
of his oldest friends.

'You mean to dance?' said Wardle.

'Of course I do,' replied Mr. Pickwick. 'Don't you see I am
dressed for the purpose?' Mr. Pickwick called attention to his
speckled silk stockings, and smartly-tied pumps.

'*You* in silk stockings!' exclaimed Mr. Tupman jocosely.

'And why not, sir—why not?' said Mr. Pickwick, turning
warmly upon him.

'Oh, of course there is no reason why you shouldn't wear them,'
responded Mr. Tupman.

'I imagine not, sir, I imagine not,' said Mr. Pickwick in a very
peremptory tone.

Mr. Tupman had contemplated a laugh, but he found it was a serious matter; so he looked grave, and said they were a pretty pattern.

'I hope they are,' said Mr. Pickwick fixing his eyes upon his friend. 'You see nothing extraordinary in the stockings, *as* stockings, I trust, sir?'

'Certainly not. Oh, certainly not,' replied Mr. Tupman. He walked away; and Mr. Pickwick's countenance resumed its customary benign expression.

'We are all ready, I believe,' said Mr. Pickwick, who was stationed with the old lady at the top of the dance, and had already made four false starts, in his excessive anxiety to commence.

'Then begin at once,' said Wardle. 'Now!'

Up struck the two fiddles and the one harp, and off went Mr. Pickwick into hands across, when there was a general clapping of hands, and a cry of 'Stop, stop!'

'What's the matter!' said Mr. Pickwick, who was only brought to, by the fiddles and harp desisting, and could have been stopped by no other earthly power, if the house had been on fire.

'Where's Arabella Allen?' cried a dozen voices.

'And Winkle?' added Mr. Tupman.

'Here we are!' exclaimed that gentleman, emerging with his pretty companion from the corner; as he did so, it would have been hard to tell which was the redder in the face, he or the young lady with the black eyes.

'What an extraordinary thing it is, Winkle,' said Mr. Pickwick, rather pettishly, 'that you couldn't have taken your place before.'

'Not at all extraordinary,' said Mr. Winkle.

'Well,' said Mr. Pickwick, with a very expressive smile, as his eyes rested on Arabella, 'well, I don't know that it *was* extraordinary, either, after all.'

However, there was no time to think more about the matter, for the fiddles and harp began in real earnest. Away went Mr. Pickwick—hands across—down the middle to the very end of the room, and half-way up the chimney, back again to the door—

poussette everywhere—loud stamp on the ground—ready for the next couple—off again—all the figure over once more—another stamp to beat out the time—next couple, and the next, and the next again—never was such going! At last, after they had reached the bottom of the dance, and full fourteen couple after the old lady had retired in an exhausted state, and the clergyman's wife had been substituted in her stead, did that gentleman, when there was no demand whatever on his exertions, keep perpetually dancing in his place, to keep time to the music: smiling on his partner all the while with a blandness of demeanour which baffles all description.

Long before Mr. Pickwick was weary of dancing, the newly-married couple had retired from the scene. There was a glorious supper down-stairs, notwithstanding, and a good long sitting after it; and when Mr. Pickwick awoke, late the next morning, he had a confused recollection of having, severally and confidentially, invited somewhere about five-and-forty people to dine with him at the George and Vulture, the very first time they came to London; which Mr. Pickwick rightly considered a pretty certain indication of his having taken something besides exercise, on the previous night.

'And so your family has games in the kitchen to-night, my dear, has they?' inquired Sam of Emma.

'Yes, Mr. Weller,' replied Emma; 'we always have on Christmas eve. Master wouldn't neglect to keep it up on any account.'

'Your master's a wery pretty notion of keepin' anythin' up, my dear,' said Mr. Weller; 'I never see such a sensible sort of man as he is, or such a reg'lar gen'l'm'n.'

'Oh, that he is!' said the fat boy, joining in the conversation; 'don't he breed nice pork!' The fat youth gave a semi-cannibalic leer at Mr. Weller, as he thought of the roast legs and gravy.

'Oh, you've woke up, at last, have you?' said Sam.

The fat boy nodded.

'I'll tell you what it is, young boa constructer,' said Mr. Weller, impressively; 'if you don't sleep a little less, and exercise a little more, wen you comes to be a man you'll lay yourself open to the same sort of personal inconwenience as was inflicted on the old gen'l'm'n as wore the pigtail.'

'What did they do to him?' inquired the fat boy, in a faltering voice.

'I'm a-goin' to tell you,' replied Mr. Weller; 'he was one o' the largest patterns as was ever turned out—reg'lar fat man, as hadn't caught a glimpse of his own shoes for five-and-forty year.'

'Lor!' exclaimed Emma.

'No, that he hadn't, my dear,' said Mr. Weller; 'and if you'd put an exact model of his own legs on the dinin' table afore him, he wouldn't ha' known 'em. Well, he always walks to his office with a wery handsome gold watch-chain hanging out, about a foot and a quarter, and a gold watch in his fob pocket as was worth—I'm afraid to say how much, but as much as a watch can be—a large, heavy, round manafacter, as stout for a watch, as he was for a man, and with a big face in proportion. "You'd better not carry that 'ere watch," says the old gen'l'm'n's friends, "you'll be robbed on it," says they. "Shall I?" says he. "Yes, you will," says they. "Vell," says he, "I should like to see the thief as could get this here watch out, for I'm blest if *I* ever can, it's such a tight fit," says he; "and venever I wants to know what's o'clock, I'm obliged to stare into the bakers' shops," he says. Well, then he laughs as hearty as if he was a goin' to pieces, and out he walks agin' with his powdered head and pigtail, and rolls down the Strand vith the chain hangin' out furder than ever, and the great round watch almost bustin' through his grey kersey smalls. There warn't a pickpocket in all London as didn't take a pull at that chain, but the chain 'ud never break, and the watch 'ud never come out, so they soon got tired o' dragging such a heavy old gen'l'm'n along the pavement, and he'd go home and laugh till the pigtail wibrated like the penderlum of a Dutch clock. At last, one day the old gen'l'm'n was a rollin' along, and he sees a pickpocket as he know'd by sight, a-comin' up, arm in arm vith a little boy with a wery large head. "Here's a game," says the old gen'l'm'n to himself, "they're a-goin' to have another try, but it

won't do!" So he begins a-chucklin' wery hearty, wen, all of a
sudden, the little boy leaves hold of the pickpocket's arm and
rushes headforemost straight into the old gen'l'm'n's stomach, and
for a moment doubles him right up vith the pain. "Murder!" says
the old gen'l'm'n. "All right, sir," says the pickpocket, a wisperin'
in his ear. And wen he come straight agin, the watch and chain was
gone, and what's worse than that, the old gen'l'm'n's digestion
was all wrong ever artervards, to the wery last day of his life; so
just you look about you, young feller, and take care you don't get
too fat.'

As Mr. Weller concluded this moral tale, with which the fat boy
appeared much affected, they all three repaired to the large kitchen,
in which the family were by this time assembled, according to
annual custom on Christmas eve, observed by old Wardle's forefa-
thers from time immemorial.

From the centre of the ceiling of this kitchen, old Wardle had just
suspended, with his own hands, a huge branch of mistletoe, and
this same branch of mistletoe instantaneously gave rise to a scene
of general and delightful struggling and confusion; in the midst of
which, Mr. Pickwick, with a gallantry that would have done honour to a descendant of Lady Tollimglower herself, took the old lady
by the hand, led her beneath the mystic branch, and saluted her in
all courtesy and decorum. The old lady submitted to this piece of
practical politeness with all the dignity which befitted so important
and serious a solemnity, but the younger ladies, not being so thoroughly imbued with a superstitious veneration for the custom: or
imagining that the value of a salute is very much enhanced if it cost
a little trouble to obtain it: screamed and struggled, and ran into
corners, and threatened and remonstrated, and did everything but
leave the room, until some of the less adventurous gentlemen were
on the point of desisting, when they all at once found it useless to
resist any longer, and submitted to be kissed with a good grace. Mr.
Winkle kissed the young lady with the black eyes, and Mr.
Snodgrass kissed Emily, and Mr. Weller, not being particular about

the form of being under the mistletoe, kissed Emma and the other female servants, just as he caught them. As to the poor relations, they kissed everybody, not even excepting the plainer portions of the young-lady visitors, who, in their excessive confusion, ran right under the mistletoe, as soon as it was hung up, without knowing it! Wardle stood with his back to the fire, surveying the whole scene, with the utmost satisfaction; and the fat boy took the opportunity of appropriating to his own use, and summarily devouring, a particularly fine mince-pie, that had been carefully put by for somebody else.

Now, the screaming had subsided, and faces were in a glow, and curls in a tangle, and Mr. Pickwick, after kissing the old lady as before mentioned, was standing under the mistletoe, looking with a very pleased countenance on all that was passing around him, when the young lady with the black eyes, after a little whispering with the other young ladies, made a sudden dart forward, and, putting her arm round Mr. Pickwick's neck, saluted him affectionately on the left cheek; and before Mr. Pickwick distinctly knew what was the matter, he was surrounded by the whole body, and kissed by every one of them.

It was a pleasant thing to see Mr. Pickwick, in the centre of the group, now pulled this way, and then that, and first kissed on the chin, and then on the nose, and then on the spectacles: and to hear the peals of laughter which were raised on every side; but it was a still more pleasant thing to see Mr. Pickwick, blinded shortly afterwards with a silk handkerchief, falling up against the wall, and scrambling into corners, and going through all the mysteries of blind-man's buff, with the utmost relish for the game, until at last he caught one of the poor relations, and then had to evade the blind-man himself, which he did with a nimbleness and agility that elicited the admiration and applause of all beholders. The poor relations caught the people who they thought would like it, and, when the game flagged, got caught themselves. When they were all tired of blind-man's buff, there was a great game at snap-dragon, and when fingers enough were burned with that, and all the raisins were gone, they sat down by the huge fire of blazing logs to a substantial supper, and a mighty bowl of wassail, something smaller than an ordinary wash-house copper, in which the hot apples were hissing and bubbling with a rich look, and a jolly sound, that were perfectly irresistible.

'This,' said Mr. Pickwick, looking round him, 'this is, indeed, comfort.'

'Our invariable custom,' replied Mr. Wardle. 'Everybody sits down with us on Christmas eve, as you see them now—servants and all; and here we wait, until the clock strikes twelve, to usher Christmas in, and beguile the time with forfeits and old stories. Trundle, my boy, rake up the fire.'

Up flew the bright sparks in myriads as the logs were stirred. The deep red blaze sent forth a rich glow, that penetrated into the farthest corner of the room, and cast its cheerful tint on every face.

'Come,' said Wardle, 'a song—a Christmas song! I'll give you one, in default of a better.'

'Bravo!' said Mr. Pickwick.

'Fill up,' cried Wardle. 'It will be two hours, good, before you see the bottom of the bowl through the deep rich colour of the wassail; fill up all round, and now for the song.'

Thus saying, the merry old gentleman, in a good, round, sturdy voice, commenced without more ado:

A CHRISTMAS CAROL

I CARE not for Spring; on his fickle wing
Let the blossoms and buds be borne:
He woos them amain with his treacherous rain,
And he scatters them ere the morn.
An inconstant elf, he knows not himself,
Nor his own changing mind an hour,
He'll smile in your face, and, with wry grimace,
He'll wither your youngest flower.

Let the Summer sun to his bright home run,
He shall never be sought by me;
When he's dimmed by a cloud I can laugh aloud,
And care not how sulky he be!
For his darling child is the madness wild
That sports in fierce fever's train;
And when love is too strong, it don't last long,
As many have found to their pain.

A mild harvest night, by the tranquil light
Of the modest and gentle moon,
Has a far sweeter sheen, for me, I ween,
Than the broad and unblushing noon.
But every leaf awakens my grief,
As it lieth beneath the tree;
So let Autumn air be never so fair,
It by no means agrees with me.

But my song I troll out, for CHRISTMAS stout,
The hearty, the true, and the bold;
A bumper I drain, and with might and main
Give three cheers for this Christmas old!
We'll usher him in with a merry din
That shall gladden his joyous heart,
And we'll keep him up, while there's bite or sup,
And in fellowship good, we'll part.

In his fine honest pride, he scorns to hide,
One jot of his hard-weather scars;
They're no disgrace, for there's much the same trace
On the cheeks of our bravest tars.
Then again I sing 'till the roof doth ring,
And it echoes from wall to wall—
To the stout old wight, fair welcome to-night,
As the King of the Seasons all!

This song was tumultuously applauded—for friends and dependents make a capital audience—and the poor relations, especially, were in perfect ecstasies of rapture. Again was the fire replenished, and again went the wassail round.

'How it snows!' said one of the men, in a low tone.

'Snows, does it?' said Wardle.

'Rough, cold night, sir,' replied the man; 'and there's a wind got up, that drifts it across the fields, in a thick white cloud.'

'What does Jem say?' inquired the old lady. 'There ain't anything the matter, is there?'

'No, no, mother,' replied Wardle; 'he says there's a snow-drift, and a wind that's piercing cold. I should know that, by the way it rumbles in the chimney.'

'Ah!' said the old lady, 'there was just such a wind, and just such a fall of snow, a good many years back, I recollect—just five years before your poor father died. It was a Christmas eve, too; and I remember that on that very night he told us the story about the goblins that carried away old Gabriel Grub.'

'The story about what?' said Mr. Pickwick.

'Oh, nothing, nothing,' replied Wardle. 'About an old sexton, that the good people down here suppose to have been carried away by goblins.'

'Suppose!' ejaculated the old lady. 'Is there any body hardy enough to disbelieve it? Suppose! Haven't you heard ever since you were a child, that he *was* carried away by the goblins, and don't you know he was?'

'Very well, mother, he was, if you like,' said Wardle, laughing. 'He *was* carried away by goblins, Pickwick; and there's an end of the matter.'

'No, no,' said Mr. Pickwick, 'not an end of it, I assure you; for I must hear how, and why, and all about it.'

Wardle smiled, as every head was bent forward to hear; and filling out the wassail with no stinted hand, nodded a health to Mr. Pickwick, and began as follows:

"The Story of the Goblins
Who Stole a Sexton"

'In an old abbey town, down in this part of the country, a long, long while ago—so long, that the story must be a true one, because our great grandfathers implicitly believed it— there officiated as sexton and grave-digger in the churchyard, one Gabriel Grub. It by no means follows that because a man is a sexton, and constantly surrounded by the emblems of mortality, therefore he should be a morose and melancholy man; your undertakers are the merriest fellows in the world; and I once had the honour of being on intimate terms with a mute, who in private life, and off duty, was as comical and jocose a little fellow as ever chirped out a devil-may-care song, without a hitch in his memory, or drained off the contents of a good stiff glass without stopping for breath. But, notwith- standing these precedents to the contrary, Gabriel Grub was an ill-conditioned, cross-grained, surly fellow—a morose and lonely man, who consorted with nobody but himself, and an old wicker bottle which fitted into his large deep waistcoat pocket—and who eyed each merry face, as it passed him by, with such a deep scowl of malice and ill-humour, as it was difficult to meet, without feeling something the worse for.

'A little before twilight, one Christmas Eve, Gabriel shoul- dered his spade, lighted his lantern, and betook himself to- wards the old churchyard; for he had got a grave to finish by next morning, and, feeling very low, he thought it might raise his spirits, perhaps, if he went on with his work at once. As he went his way, up the ancient street, he saw the cheerful light of the blazing fires gleam through the old casements, and heard the loud laugh and the cheerful shouts of those who were assembled around them; he marked the bustling preparations for next day's cheer, and smelt the numerous savoury odours consequent thereupon, as they steamed up from the kitchen windows in clouds. All this was gall and wormwood to the heart of Gabriel Grub; and when groups of children bounded out of the houses, tripped across the road, and were met, before they could knock at the opposite door, by half a dozen curly-headed little rascals who crowded round them as they flocked up-stairs to spend the evening in their Christmas games, Gabriel smiled grimly, and clutched the handle of his spade with a firmer grasp, as he thought of measles, scarlet-fever, thrush, hooping-cough, and a good many other sources of consolation besides.

'In this happy frame of mind, Gabriel strode along: returning a short, sullen growl to the good-humoured greetings of such of his neighbours as now and then passed him: until he turned into the dark lane which led to the churchyard. Now, Gabriel had been looking forward to reaching the dark lane, because it was, generally speaking, a nice, gloomy, mournful place, into which the towns-people did not much care to go, except in broad daylight, and when the sun was shining; consequently, he was not a little indignant to hear a young urchin roaring out some jolly song about a merry Christmas, in this very sanctuary, which had been called Coffin Lane ever since the days of the old abbey, and the time of the shaven-headed monks. As Gabriel walked on, and the voice drew nearer, he found it proceeded from a small boy, who was hurrying along, to join one of the little parties in the old street, and who, partly to keep himself company, and partly to prepare himself for the occasion, was shouting out the song at the highest pitch of his lungs. So Gabriel waited until the boy came up, and then dodged him into a corner, and rapped him over the head with his lantern five or six times, to teach him to modulate his voice. And as the boy hurried away with his hand to his head, singing quite a different sort of tune, Gabriel Grub chuckled very heartily to himself, and entered the churchyard: locking the gate behind him.

'He took off his coat, put down his lantern, and getting into the unfinished grave, worked at it for an hour or so, with right good will. But the earth was hardened with the frost, and it was no very easy matter to break it up, and shovel it out; and although there was a moon, it was a very young one, and shed little light upon the grave, which was in the shadow of the church. At any other time, these obstacles would have made Gabriel Grub very moody and miserable, but he was so well pleased with having stopped the small boy's singing, that he took little heed of the scanty progress he had made, and looked down into the grave, when he had finished work for the night, with grim satisfaction: murmuring as he gathered up his things:

> Brave lodgings for one, brave lodgings for one,
> A few feet of cold earth, when life is done;
> A stone at the head, a stone at the feet,
> A rich, juicy meal for the worms to eat;
> Rank grass over head, and damp clay around,
> Brave lodgings for one, these, in holy ground!

' "Ho! ho!" laughed Gabriel Grub, as he sat himself down on a flat tombstone which was a favourite resting-place of his; and drew forth his wicker bottle. "A coffin at Christmas! A Christmas Box. Ho! ho! ho!"

' "Ho! ho! ho!" repeated a voice which sounded close behind him.

'Gabriel paused, in some alarm, in the act of raising the wicker bottle to his lips: and looked round. The bottom of the oldest grave about him, was not more still and quiet, than the churchyard in the pale moonlight. The cold hoar-frost glistened on the tombstones, and sparkled like rows of gems, among the stone carvings of the old church. The snow lay hard and crisp upon the ground; and spread over the thickly-strewn mounds of earth so white and smooth a cover that it seemed as if corpses lay there, hidden only by their winding sheets. Not the faintest rustle broke the profound tranquillity of the solemn scene. Sound itself appeared to be frozen up, all was so cold and still.

' "It was the echoes," said Gabriel Grub, raising the bottle to his lips again.

' "It was *not*," said a deep voice.

'Gabriel started up, and stood rooted to the spot with astonishment and terror; for his eyes rested on a form that made his blood run cold.

'Seated on an upright tombstone, close to him, was a strange unearthly figure, whom Gabriel felt at once, was no being of this world. His long fantastic legs which might have reached the ground, were cocked up, and crossed after a quaint, fantastic fashion; his sinewy arms were bare; and his hands rested on his knees. On his short round body, he wore a close covering, ornamented with small slashes; a short cloak dangled at his back; the collar was cut into curious peaks, which served the goblin in lieu of ruff or neckerchief; and his shoes curled up at his toes into long points. On his head, he wore a broad-brimmed sugar-loaf hat, garnished with a single feather. The hat was covered with the white frost; and the goblin looked as if he had sat on the same tombstone very comfortably, for two or three hundred years. He was sitting perfectly still; his tongue was put out, as if in derision; and he was grinning at Gabriel Grub with such a grin as only a goblin could call up.

' "It was *not* the echoes," said the goblin.

'Gabriel Grub was paralysed, and could make no reply.

' "What do you do here on Christmas Eve?" said the goblin sternly.

' "I came to dig a grave, sir," stammered Gabriel Grub.

' "What man wanders among graves and churchyards on such a night as this?" cried the goblin.

' "Gabriel Grub! Gabriel Grub!" screamed a wild chorus of voices that seemed to fill the churchyard. Gabriel looked fearfully round—nothing was to be seen.

' "What have you got in that bottle?" said the goblin.

' "Hollands, sir," replied the sexton, trembling more than ever; for he had bought it of the smugglers, and he thought that perhaps his questioner might be in the excise department of the goblins.

' "Who drinks Hollands alone, and in a churchyard, on such a night as this?" said the goblin.

' "Gabriel Grub! Gabriel Grub!" exclaimed the wild voices again.

'The goblin leered maliciously at the terrified sexton, and then raising his voice, exclaimed:

' "And who, then, is our fair and lawful prize?"

'To this inquiry the invisible chorus replied, in a strain that sounded like the voices of many choristers singing to the mighty swell of the old church organ—a strain that seemed borne to the sexton's ears upon a wild wind, and to die away as it passed onward; but the burden of the reply was still the same, "Gabriel Grub! Gabriel Grub!"

'The goblin grinned a broader grin than before, as he said, "Well Gabriel, what do you say to this?"

'The sexton gasped for breath.

' "What do you think of this, Gabriel?" said the goblin, kicking up his feet in the air on either side of the tombstone, and looking at the turned-up points with as much complacency as if he had been contemplating the most fashionable pair of Wellingtons in all Bond Street.

' "It's—it's—very curious, sir," replied the sexton, half dead with fright; "very curious, and very pretty, but I think I'll go back and finish my work, sir, if you please."

' "Work!" said the goblin, "what work?"

' "The grave, sir; making the grave," stammered the sexton.

' "Oh, the grave, eh?" said the goblin; "who makes graves at a time when all other men are merry, and takes a pleasure in it?"

'Again the mysterious voices replied, "Gabriel Grub! Gabriel Grub!"

' "I'm afraid my friends want you, Gabriel," said the goblin, thrusting his tongue farther into his cheek than ever—and a most astonishing tongue it was—"I'm afraid my friends want you, Gabriel," said the goblin.

' "Under favour, sir," replied the horror-stricken sexton, "I don't think they can, sir; they don't know me, sir; I don't think the gentlemen have ever seen me, sir."

' "Oh yes they have," replied the goblin; "we know the man with the sulky face and grim scowl, that came down the street to-night, throwing his evil looks at the children, and grasping his burying spade the tighter. We know the man who struck the boy in the envious malice of his heart, because the boy could be merry, and he could not. We know him, we know him."

'Here, the goblin gave a loud shrill laugh, which the echoes returned twenty-fold: and throwing his legs up in the air, stood upon his head, or rather upon the very point of his sugar-loaf hat, on the narrow edge of the tombstone: whence he threw a somerset with extraordinary agility, right to the sexton's feet, at which he planted himself in the attitude in which tailors generally sit upon the shop-board.

' "I—I—am afraid I must leave you, sir," said the sexton, making an effort to move.

' "Leave us!" said the goblin, "Gabriel Grub going to leave us. Ho! ho! ho!"

'As the goblin laughed, the sexton observed, for one instant, a brilliant illumination within the windows of the church, as if the whole building were lighted up; it disappeared, the organ pealed forth a lively air, and whole troops of goblins, the very counterpart of the first one, poured into the churchyard, and began playing at leap-frog with the tombstones; never stopping for an instant to take breath, but "overing" the highest among them, one after the other, with the most marvellous dexterity. The first goblin was a most astonishing leaper, and none of the others could come near him; even in the extremity of his terror the sexton could not help observing, that while his friends were content to leap over the common-sized gravestones, the first one took the family vaults, iron railings and all, with as much ease as if they had been so many street posts.

'At last the game reached to a most exciting pitch; the organ played quicker and quicker; and the goblins leaped faster and faster: coiling themselves up, rolling head over heels upon the ground, and bounding over the tombstones like footballs. The sexton's brain whirled round with the rapidity of the motion he beheld, and his legs reeled beneath him, as the spirits flew before his eyes: when the goblin king, suddenly darting towards him, laid his hand upon his collar, and sank with him through the earth.

'When Gabriel Grub had had time to fetch his breath, which the rapidity of his descent had for the moment taken away, he found himself in what appeared to be a large cavern, surrounded on all sides by crowds of goblins, ugly and grim; in the centre of the room, on an elevated seat, was stationed his friend of the churchyard; and close beside him stood Gabriel Grub himself, without power of motion.

' "Cold to-night," said the king of the goblins, "very cold. A glass of something warm, here!"

'At this command, half a dozen officious goblins, with a perpetual smile upon their faces, whom Gabriel Grub imagined to be courtiers, on that account, hastily disappeared, and presently returned with a goblet of liquid fire, which they presented to the king.

' "Ah!" cried the goblin, whose cheeks and throat were transparent, as he tossed down the flame, "This warms one, indeed! Bring a bumper of the same, for Mr. Grub."

'It was in vain for the unfortunate sexton to protest that he was not in the habit of taking anything warm at night; one of the goblins held him while another poured the blazing liquid down his throat; the whole assembly screeched with laughter as he coughed and choked, and wiped away the tears which gushed plentifully from his eyes, after swallowing the burning draught.

' "And now," said the king, fantastically poking the taper corner of his sugar-loaf hat into the sexton's eye, and thereby occasioning him the most exquisite pain: "And now, show the man of misery and gloom, a few of the pictures from our own great storehouse!"

'As the goblin said this, a thick cloud which obscured the remoter end of the cavern, rolled gradually away, and disclosed, apparently at a great distance, a small and scantily furnished, but neat and clean apartment. A crowd of little children were gathered round a bright fire, clinging to their mother's gown, and gambolling around her chair. The mother occasionally rose, and drew aside the window-curtain, as if to look for some expected object: a frugal meal was ready spread upon the table; and an elbow chair was placed near the fire. A knock was heard at the door: the mother opened it, and the children crowded round her, and clapped their hands for joy, as their father entered. He was wet and weary, and shook the snow from his garments, as the children crowded round him, and seizing his cloak, hat, stick, and gloves, with busy zeal, ran with them from the room. Then, as he sat down to his meal before the fire, the children climbed about his knee, and the mother sat by his side, and all seemed happiness and comfort.

'But a change came upon the view, almost imperceptibly. The scene was altered to a small bed-room, where the fairest and youngest child lay dying: the roses had fled from his cheek, and the light from his eye; and even as the sexton looked upon him with an interest he had never felt or known before, he died. His young brothers and sisters crowded round his little bed, and seized his tiny hand, so cold and heavy; but they shrunk back from its touch, and looked with awe on his infant face; for calm and tranquil as it was, and sleeping in rest and peace as the beautiful child seemed to be, they saw that he was dead, and they knew that he was an Angel looking down upon, and blessing them, from a bright and happy Heaven.

'Again the light cloud passed across the picture, and again the subject changed. The father and mother were old and helpless now, and the number of those about them was diminished more than half; but content and cheerfulness sat on every face, and beamed in every eye, as they crowded round the fireside, and told and listened to old stories of earlier and bygone days. Slowly and peacefully, the father sank into the grave, and, soon after, the sharer of all his cares and troubles followed him to a place of rest. The few, who yet survived them, knelt by their tomb, and watered the green turf which covered it, with their tears; then rose, and turned away: sadly and mournfully, but not with bitter cries, or despairing lamentations, for they knew that they should one day meet again; and once more they mixed with the busy world, and their content and cheerfulness were restored. The cloud settled upon the picture, and concealed it from the sexton's view.

' "What do you think of *that?*" said the goblin, turning his large face towards Gabriel Grub.

'Gabriel murmured out something about its being very pretty, and looked somewhat ashamed, as the goblin bent his fiery eyes upon him.

' "*You* a miserable man!" said the goblin, in a tone of excessive contempt. "You!" He appeared disposed to add more, but indignation choked his utterance, so he lifted up one of his very pliable legs, and flourishing it above his head a little, to insure his aim, administered a good sound kick to Gabriel Grub; immediately after which, all the goblins in waiting, crowded round the wretched sexton, and kicked him without mercy: according to the established and invariable custom of courtiers upon earth, who kick whom royalty kicks, and hug whom royalty hugs.

'"Show him some more!" said the king of the goblins.

'At these words, the cloud was dispelled, and rich and beautiful landscape was disclosed to view—there is just such another, to this day, within a half a mile of the old abbey town. The sun shone from out the clear blue sky, the water sparkled beneath his rays, and the trees looked greener, and the flowers more gay, beneath his cheering influence. The water rippled on, with a pleasant sound; the trees rustled in the light wind that murmured among their leaves; the birds sang upon the boughs; and the lark carolled on high her welcome to the morning. Yes, it was morning; the bright, balmy morning of summer; the minutest leaf, the smallest blade of grass, was instinct with life. The ant crept forth to her daily toil, the butterfly fluttered and basked in the warm rays of the sun; myriads of insects spread their transparent wings, and revelled in their brief but happy existence. Man walked forth, elated with the scene; and all was brightness and splendour.

'"*You* a miserable man!" said the king of the goblins, in a more contemptuous tone than before. And again the king of the goblins gave his leg a flourish; again it descended on the shoulders of the sexton; and again the attendant goblins imitated the example of their chief.

'Many a time the cloud went and came, and many a lesson it taught to Gabriel Grub, who, although his shoulders smarted with pain from the frequent applications of the goblins' feet, looked on with an interest that nothing could diminish. He saw that men who worked hard, and earned their scanty bread with lives of labour, were cheerful and happy; and that to the most ignorant, the sweet face of nature was a never-failing source of cheerfulness and joy. He saw those who had been delicately nurtured, and tenderly brought up, cheerful under privation, and superior to suffering that would have crushed many of a rougher grain, because they bore within their own bosoms the materials of happiness, contentment, and peace. He saw that women, the tenderest and most fragile of all God's creatures, were the oftenest superior to sorrow, adversity, and distress; and he saw that it was because they bore, in their own hearts, an inexhaustible well-spring of affection and devotion. Above all, he saw that men like himself, who snarled at the mirth and cheerfulness of others, were the foulest weeds on the fair surface of the earth; and setting all the good of the world against the evil, he came to the conclusion that it was a very decent and respectable sort of world after all. No sooner had he formed it, than the cloud which closed over the last picture, seemed to settle on his senses, and lull him to repose. One by one, the goblins faded from his sight; and as the last one disappeared, he sunk into sleep.

'The day had broken when Gabriel Grub awoke, and found himself lying, at full length on the flat gravestone in the churchyard, with the wicker bottle lying empty by his side, and his coat, spade, and lantern, all well whitened by the last night's frost, scattered on the ground. The stone on which he had first seen the goblin seated, stood bolt upright before him, and the grave at which he had worked, the night before, was not far off. At first, he began to doubt the reality of his adventures, but the acute pain in his shoulders when he attempted to rise, assured him that the kicking of the goblins was certainly not ideal. He was staggered again, by observing no traces of footsteps in the snow on which the goblins had played at leap-frog with the gravestones, but he speedily accounted for this circumstance when he remembered that, being spirits, they would leave no visible impression behind them. So, Gabriel Grub got on his feet as well as he could, for the pain in his back; and brushing the frost off his coat, put it on, and turned his face towards the town.

'But he was an altered man, and he could not bear the thought of returning to a place where his repentance would be scoffed at, and his reformation disbelieved. He hesitated for a few moments; and then turned away to wander where he might, and seek his bread elsewhere.

'The lantern, the spade, and the wicker bottle, were found, that day, in the churchyard. There were a great many speculations about the sexton's fate, at first, but it was speedily determined that he had been carried away by the goblins; and there were not wanting some very credible witnesses who had distinctly seen him whisked through the air on the back of a chestnut horse blind of one eye, with the hind-quarters of a lion, and the tail of a bear. At length all this was devoutly believed; and the new sexton used to exhibit to the curious, for a trifling emolument, a good-sized piece of the church weathercock which had been accidentally kicked off by the aforesaid horse in his aerial flight, and picked up by himself in the churchyard, a year or two afterwards.

'Unfortunately, these stories were somewhat disturbed by the unlooked-for re-appearance of Gabriel Grub himself, some ten years afterwards, a ragged, contented, rheumatic old man. He told his story to the clergyman, and also to the mayor; and in course of time it began to be received, as a matter of history, in which form it has continued down to this very day. The believers in the weathercock tale, having misplaced their confidence once, were not easily prevailed upon to part with it again, so they looked as wise as they could, shrugged their shoulders, touched their foreheads, and murmured something about Gabriel Grub having drunk all the Hollands, and then fallen asleep on the flat tombstone; and they affected to explain what he supposed he had witnessed in the goblin's cavern, by saying that he had seen the world, and grown wiser. But this opinion, which was by no means a popular one at any time, gradually died off; and be the matter how it may, as Gabriel Grub was afflicted with rheumatism to the end of his days, this story has at least one moral, if it teach no better one—and that is, that if a man turn sulky and drink by himself at Christmas time, he may make up his mind to be not a bit the better for it: let the spirits be never so good, or let them be even as many degrees beyond proof, as those which Gabriel Grub saw in the goblin's cavern.'

The Cricket
on the
Hearth

*The kettle had had the last of its solo performance. It persevered with
undiminished ardour; but the Cricket took first fiddle and kept it. Good
Heaven, how it chirped! Its shrill, sharp, piercing voice resounded through
the house, and seemed to twinkle in the outer darkness like a star. . . . They
went very well together, the Cricket and the kettle. The burden of the song
was still the same; and louder, louder, louder still, they sang it in their
emulation.*

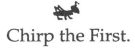

Chirp the First.

The kettle began it! Don't tell me what Mrs. Peerybingle
said. I know better. Mrs. Peerybingle may leave it on
record to the end of time that she couldn't say which
of them began it; but, I say the kettle did. I ought to
know, I hope! The kettle began it, full five minutes by the little
waxy-faced Dutch clock in the corner, before the Cricket uttered a
chirp.

Let me narrate exactly how it happened. It appeared as if there
were a sort of match, or trial of skill, you must understand, between the kettle and the Cricket. And this is what led to it, and how
it came about.

Mrs. Peerybingle, going out into the raw twilight, and clicking
over the wet stones in a pair of pattens that worked innumerable
rough impressions of the first proposition in Euclid all about the
yard—Mrs. Peerybingle filled the kettle at the water-butt.

The kettle was aggravating and obstinate. It wouldn't allow itself to be adjusted on the top bar; it wouldn't hear of accommodating itself kindly to the knobs of coal; it *would* lean forward with a drunken air, and dribble, a very Idiot of a kettle, on the hearth. It was quarrelsome, and hissed and spluttered morosely at the fire. To sum up all the lid, resisting Mrs. Peerybingle's fingers, first of all turned topsy-turvy, and then, with an ingenious pertinacity deserving of a better cause, dived sideways in—down to the very bottom of the kettle. And the hull of the Royal George has never made half the monstrous resistance to coming out of the water, which the lid of that kettle employed against Mrs. Peerybingle, before she got up again.

But, Mrs. Peerybingle, with good-humor, dusted her chubby little hands against each other, and sat down before the kettle, laughing. Meantime, the jolly blaze uprose and fell, flashing and gleaming on the little Haymaker at the top of the Dutch clock, until one might have thought he stood stock still before the Moorish Palace, and nothing was in motion but the flame. He was on the move, however; and had his spasms, two to the second, all right and regular.

Now it was, you observe, that the kettle began to spend the evening. Now it was, that the kettle, growing mellow and musical, began to have irrepressible gurglings in its throat, and to indulge in short vocal snorts, which it checked in the bud, as if it hadn't quite made up its mind yet to be good company. Now it was, that after two or three such vain attempts to stifle its convivial sentiments, it threw off all moroseness, all reserve, and burst into a stream of song so cozy and hilarious, as never maudling nightingale yet formed the least idea of.

With its warm breath gushing forth in a light cloud which merrily and gracefully ascended, a few feet, then hung about the chimney-corner as its own domestic Heaven, it trolled its song with that strong energy of cheerfulness, that its iron body hummed and stirred upon the fire; and the lid itself, the recently rebellious lid—such is the influence of a bright example—performed a sort of jig.

That this song of the kettle's was a song of invitation and welcome to somebody out of doors: to somebody at that moment;
coming on, towards the snug small home and the crisp fire: there is
no doubt whatever. Mrs. Peerybingle knew it, perfectly, as she sat
musing before the hearth. It's a dark night, sang the kettle, and
there's hoar-frost on the fingerpost, and thaw upon the track; and
the ice it isn't water, and the water isn't free; and you couldn't say
that anything is what it ought to be; but he is coming, coming,
coming!——

And here, if you like, the Cricket DID chime in! with a Chirrup,
Chirrup, Chirrup of such magnitude, by way of chorus; with a
voice so astoundingly disproportionate to its size, as compared
with the kettle; (size! you couldn't see it!) that if it had then and
there burst itself like an overcharged gun, if it had fallen a victim
on the spot and chirruped its little body into fifty pieces, it would
have seemed a natural and inevitable consequence, for which it
had expressly labored.

The kettle had had the last of its solo performance. It persevered
with undiminished ardor; but the Cricket took first fiddle and kept
it. Good Heaven, how it chirped! Its shrill, sharp, piercing voice
resounded through the house, and seemed to twinkle in the outer
darkness like a star. There was an indescribable little trill and trem-
ble in it, at it loudest, which suggested its being carried off its legs,
and made to leap again, by its own intense enthusiasm. Yet they
went very well together, the Cricket and the kettle. The burden of
the song was still the same; and louder, louder, louder still, they
sang it in their emulation.

The fair little listener—for fair she was, and young: though
something of what is called the dumpling shape; but I don't myself
object to that—lighted a candle, glanced at the Haymaker on the
top of the clock, who was getting in a pretty average crop of minutes; and looked out of the window, where she saw nothing, owing
to the darkness, but her own face imaged in the glass. And my
opinion is (and so would yours have been), that she might have
looked a long way, and seen nothing half so agreeable. When she

came back, and sat down in her former seat, the Cricket and the kettle were still keeping it up, with a perfect fury of competition. The kettle's weak side clearly being, that he didn't know when he was beat.

There was all the excitement of a race about it. Chirp, chirp, chirp! Cricket a mile ahead. Hum, hum, hum—m—m! Kettle making play in the distance, like a great top. Chirp, chirp, chirp! Cricket round the corner. Hum, hum, hum—m—m! Kettle sticking to him in his own way; no idea of giving in. Chirp, chirp, chirp! Cricket fresher than ever. Hum, hum, hum—m—m! Kettle slow and steady. Chirp, chirp, chirp! Cricket going to finish him. Hum, hum, hum—m—m! Kettle not to be finished. Until at last they get so jumbled together, in the hurry-skurry, helter-skelter, of the match, that whether the kettle chirped and the Cricket hummed, or the Cricket chirped and the kettle hummed, or they both chirped and both hummed, it would have taken a clearer head than yours or mine to have decided with anything like certainty. But, of this there is no doubt: that, the kettle and the Cricket, at one and the same moment, and by some power of amalgamation best known to themselves, sent, each, his fireside song of comfort streaming into a ray of the candle that shone out through the window, and a long way down the lane. And this light, bursting on a certain person who, on the instant, approached towards it through the gloom, expressed the whole thing to him, literally in a twinkling, and cried, "Welcome home, old fellow! Welcome home, my boy!"

This end attained, the kettle, being dead beat, boiled over, and was taken off the fire. Mrs. Peerybingle then went running to the door, where, what with the wheels of a cart, the tramp of a horse, the voice of a man, the tearing in and out of an excited dog, and the surprising and mysterious appearance of a baby, there was soon the very What's-his-name to pay.

Where the baby came from, or how Mrs. Peerybingle got hold of it in that flash of time, I don't know. But a live baby there was, in Mrs. Peerybingle's arms; and a pretty tolerable amount of pride she seemed to have in it, when she was drawn gently to the fire, by a sturdy figure of a man, much taller and much older than herself, who had to stoop a long way down, to kiss her. But she was worth the trouble. Six foot six, with the lumbago, might have done it.

"Oh goodness, John!" said Mrs. P. "What a state you are in with the weather!"

He was something the worse for it, undeniably. The thick mist hung in clots upon his eyelashes like candied thaw; and between the fog and fire together, there were rainbows in his very whiskers.

"Why, you see, Dot," John made answer, slowly, as he unrolled a shawl from about his throat; and warmed his hands; "it—it an't exactly summer weather. So, no wonder."

"I wish you wouldn't call me Dot, John, I don't like it," said Mrs. Peerybingle: pouting in a way that clearly showed she *did* like it, very much.

"Why what else are you?" returned John, looking down upon her with a smile, and giving her waist as light a squeeze as his huge hand and arm could give. "A dot and"—here he glanced at the baby—"a dot and carry—I won't say it, for fear I should spoil it; but I was very near a joke. I don't know as ever I was nearer."

He was often near to something or other very clever, by his own account: this lumbering, slow, honest John; this John so heavy, but so light of spirit; so rough upon the surface, but so gentle at the core; so dull without, so quick within; so stolid, but so good! Oh Mother Nature, give thy children the true poetry of heart that hid itself in this poor Carrier's breast—he was but a Carrier by the way—and we can bear to have them talking prose, and leading lives of prose; and bear to bless thee for their company!

It was pleasant to see Dot, with her little figure, and her baby in her arms, inclining her delicate little head just enough on one side to let it rest in an odd, half-natural, half-affected, wholly nestling and agreeable manner, on the great rugged figure of the Carrier. It was pleasant to observe how Tilly Slowboy, waiting in the background for the baby, took special cognizance (though in her earliest teens) of this grouping; and stood with her mouth and eyes wide open, and her head thrust forward, taking it in as if it were air. Nor was it less agreeable to observe how John the Carrier, reference being made by Dot to the aforesaid baby, checked his hand when on the point of touching the infant, as if he thought he might crack it; and bending down, surveyed it from a safe distance, with a kind of puzzled pride, such as an amiable mastiff might be supposed to show, if he found himself, one day, the father of a young canary.

"An't he beautiful, John? Don't he look precious in his sleep?"

"Very precious," said John. "Very much so. He generally *is* asleep, an't he?"

"Lor, John! Good gracious no!"

"Oh," said John, pondering. "I thought his eyes was generally shut. Halloa!"

"Goodness, John, how you startle one!"

'It an't right for him to turn 'em up in that way!" said that astonished Carrier, "is it?"

"You don't deserve to be a father, you don't," said Dot with all the dignity of an experienced matron. "But how should you know what little complaints children are troubled with, John!"

"It's very true, Dot," said John, pulling off his outer-coat. "I don't know much about it. I only know that I've been fighting pretty stiffly with the wind to-night. It's been blowing north-east, straight into the cart, the whole way home."

"Poor old man, so it has!" cried Mrs. Peerybingle, instantly becoming very active. "Here! Take the precious darling, Tilly, while I make myself of some use. Bless it, I could smother it with kissing it, I could! Hie then, good dog! Hie Boxer, boy! Only let me make the tea first, John; and then I'll help you with the parcels, like a busy bee."

John went out to see that the boy with the lantern which had been dancing to and fro before the door and window, like a Will o' the Wisp, took due care of the horse; who was fatter than you would quite believe, if I gave you his measure, and so old that his birthday was lost in the mists of antiquity.

"There! There's the teapot, ready on the hob!" said Dot; as briskly busy as a child at play at keeping house. "Where are you,

John? Don't let the dear child fall under the grate, Tilly, whatever you do!"

It may be noted of Miss Slowboy, in spite of her rejecting the caution with some vivacity, that she had a rare and surprising talent for getting this baby into difficulties; and had several times imperilled its short life, in a quiet way peculiarly her own. She was of a spare and straight shape, this young lady, insomuch that her garments appeared to be in constant danger of sliding off those sharp pegs, her shoulders on which they were loosely hung.

The Cricket now began to chirp again, vehemently.

"Heyday!" said John, in his slow way. "It's merrier than ever, to-night, I think."

"And it's sure to bring us good fortune, John! It always has done so. To have a Cricket on the Hearth, is the luckiest thing in all the world!"

John looked at her as if he had very nearly got the thought into his head, that she was his Cricket in chief, and he quite agreed with her. But, it was probably one of his narrow escapes, for he said nothing.

"The first time I heard its cheerful little note, John, was on that night when you brought me home—when you brought me to my new home here; its little mistress. Nearly a year ago. You recollect, John?"

O yes. John remembered. I should think so!

"Its chirp was such a welcome to me! It seemed so full of promise and encouragement. It seemed to say, you would be kind and gentle with me, and would not expect (I had a fear of that, John, then) to find an old head on the shoulders of your foolish little wife."

John thoughtfully patted one of the shoulders, and then the head, as though he would have said No, no; he had had no such expectation; and he had been quite content to take them as they were. And really he had reason. They were very comely.

"It spoke the truth, John, when it seemed to say so; for you have ever been, I am sure, the best, most considerate, the most affectionate of husbands to me. This has been a happy home, John; and I love the Cricket for its sake!"

"Why so do I then," said the Carrier. "So do I, Dot."

"I love it for the many times I have heard it, and the many thoughts its harmless music has given me. Sometimes, in the twilight, when I have felt a little solitary and downhearted, John—before baby was here to keep me company and make the house gay—when I have thought how lonely you would be if I should die; how lonely I should be if I could know that you had lost me, dear; its Chirp, Chirp, Chirp upon the hearth, has seemed to tell me of another little voice, so sweet, so very dear to me, before whose coming sound my trouble vanished like a dream. And when I used to fear—I did fear once, John, I was very young you know—that ours might prove to be an ill-assorted marriage, I being such a child, and you more like my guardian than my husband; and that you might not, however hard you tried, to be able to learn to love me, as you hoped and prayed you might; its Chirp, Chirp, Chirp has cheered me up again, and filled me with new trust and confidence. I was thinking of these things to-night, dear, when I sat expecting you; and I love the Cricket for their sake!"

"And so do I," repeated John. "But Dot? *I* hope and pray that I might learn to love you? How you talk! I had learnt that, long before I brought you here, to be the Cricket's little mistress, Dot!"

She laid her hand, an instant, on his arm, and looked up at him with an agitated face, as if she would have told him something. Next moment she was down upon her knees before the basket, speaking in a sprightly voice, and busy with the parcels.

"There are not many of them to-night, John, but I saw some goods behind the cart, just now; and though they give more trouble, perhaps, still they pay as well; so we have no reason to grumble, have we? Besides, you have been delivering, I dare say, as you came along?"

"Oh yes," John said. "A good many."

"Why what's this round box? Heart alive, John, it's a wedding-cake!"

"Yes; I called for it at the pastry-cook's."

"And it weighs I don't know what—whole hundred-weights!" cried Dot, making a great demonstration of trying to lift it. "Whose is it, John? Where is it going?"

"Read the writing on the other side," said John.

"Why, John! My Goodness, John!"

"Ah! who'd have thought it!" John returned.

"You never mean to say," pursued Dot, sitting on the floor and shaking her head at him, "that it's Gruff and Tackleton the toy-maker!"

John nodded.

Mrs. Peerybingle nodded also, fifty times at least. Not in assent—in dumb and pitying amazement, looking the good Carrier through and through, in her abstraction.

"Why, she and I were girls at the school together, John."

He might have been thinking of her, or nearly thinking of her, perhaps, as she was in that same school time. He looked upon her with a thoughtful pleasure, but he made no answer.

"And he's as old! As unlike her!—Why, how many years older than you, is Gruff and Tackleton, John?"

"How many more cups of tea shall I drink to-night at one sitting, than Gruff and Tackleton ever took in four, I wonder!" replied John, good-humoredly, as he drew a chair to the round table, and began at the cold ham. "As to eating, I eat but little; but, that little I enjoy, Dot."

Absorbed in thought, she stood there, heedless alike of the tea and John (although he called to her, and rapped the table with his knife to startle her), until he rose and touched her on the arm; when she looked at him for a moment, and hurried to her place behind the tea-board, laughing at her negligence. But not as she had laughed before. The manner and the music were quite changed.

The Cricket, too, had stopped. Somehow the room was not so cheerful as it had been. Nothing like it.

"So, these are all the parcels, are they, John?" she said, breaking a long silence, which the honest Carrier had devoted to the practical illustration of one part of his favorite sentiment—certainly enjoying what he ate, if it couldn't be admitted that he ate but little.

"That's all," said John. "Why—no—I—" laying down his knife and fork, and taking a long breath. "I declare—I've clean forgotten the old gentleman!"

"The old gentleman?"

"In the cart," said John. "He was asleep, among the straw, the last time I saw him. I've very nearly remembered him, twice, since I came in; but he went out of my head again. Holloa! Yahip there! Rouse up! That's my hearty!"

John said these latter words outside the door, wither he had hurried with the candle in his hand.

"You're such an undeniable good sleeper, sir," said John, when the old gentleman had stood, bareheaded and motionless, in the centre of the room; "that I have half a mind to ask you where the other six are—only that would be a joke, and I know I should spoil it. Very near though," murmured the Carrier, with a chuckle; "very near!"

The Stranger, who had long white hair, good features, singularly bold and well defined for an old man, and dark, bright, penetrating eyes, looked round with a smile, and saluted the Carrier's wife by gravely inclining his head. In his hand he held a great brown club or walking-stick; and striking this upon the floor, it fell asunder, and became a chair. On which he sat down, quite composedly.

"There!" said the Carrier, turning to his wife. "That's the way I found him, sitting by the roadside! Upright as a milestone. And almost as deaf."

"Sitting in the open air, John!"

"In the open air," replied the Carrier, "just at dusk. 'Carriage Paid,' he said; and gave me eighteenpence. Then he got in. And there he is."

"He's going, John, I think!"

Not at all. He was only going to speak.

"If you please, I was to be left till called for," said the Stranger mildly. "Don't mind me."

The Carrier and his wife exchanged a look of perplexity. The Stranger raised his head; and glancing from the latter to the former, said,

"Your daughter, my good friend?"

"Wife," returned John.

"Niece?" said the Stranger.

"Wife," roared John.

"Indeed?" said the Stranger. "Surely? Very young!"

"Baby, yours?"

John gave him a gigantic nod; equivalent to an answer in the affirmative, delivered through a speaking trumpet.

"Girl?"

"Bo-o-oy!" roared John.

"Also very young, eh?"

Mrs. Peerybingle instantly struck in. "Two months and three da-ays! Vaccinated just six weeks ago-o! Took very fine-ly! Considered, by the doctor, a remarkably beautiful chi-ild! Equal to the general run of children at five months o-old!"

"Hark! He's called for, sure enough," said John. "There's somebody at the door. Open it, Tilly."

Before she could reach it, however, it was opened from without; being a primitive sort of door, with a latch that any one could lift if he chose—and a good many people did choose, for all kinds of neighbors liked to have a cheerful word or two with the Carrier, though he was no great talker himself. Being opened, it gave admission to a little, meagre, thoughtful, dingy-faced man, who seemed to have made himself a great-coat from the sack-cloth covering of some old box; for, when he turned to shut the door, and keep the weather out, he disclosed upon the back of that garment, the inscription G & T in large black capitals. Also the word GLASS in bold characters.

"Good-evening John!" said the little man. "Good-evening Mum. Good-evening Tilly. Good-evening Unbeknown! How's Baby Mum? Boxer's pretty well I hope?"

"All thriving, Caleb," replied Dot. "I am sure you need only look at the dear child, for one, to know that."

"And I'm sure I need only look at you for another," said Caleb.

He didn't look at her though; he had a wandering and thoughtful eye which seemed to be always projecting itself into some other time and place, no matter what he said; a description which will equally apply to his voice.

"Or at John for another," said Caleb. "Or at Tilly, as far as that goes. Or certainly at Boxer."

"Busy just now, Caleb?" asked the Carrier.

"Why, pretty well, John," he returned, with the distraught air of a man who was casting about for the Philosopher's stone, at least. "Pretty much so. There's rather a run on Noah's Arks at present. I could have wished to improve upon the Family, but I don't see how it's to be done at the price.

The Carrier put his hand into a pocket of the coat he had taken off; and brought out, carefully preserved in moss and paper, a tiny flower pot.

"There it is!" he said, adjusting it with great care. "Not so much as a leaf damaged. Full of buds!"

Caleb's dull eye brightened, as he took it and thanked him.

"Dear, Caleb," said the Carrier. "Very dear at this season."

"Never mind that. It would be cheap to me, whatever it cost," returned the little man. "Anything else, John?"

"A small box," replied the Carrier. "Here you are!"

"'For Caleb Plummer,'" said the little man, spelling out the direction. "'With Cash.' With Cash, John? I don't think it's for me."

"With Care," returned the Carrier looking over his shoulder. "Where do you make out cash?"

"Oh! To be sure!" said Caleb. "It's all right. With care! Yes, yes; that's mine. It might have been with cash, indeed, if my dear Boy in the Golden South Americas had lived, John. You loved him as a son; didn't you. You needn't say you did. *I* know, of course. 'Caleb Plummer. With care.' Yes, yes, it's all right. It's a box of dolls' eyes for my daughter's work. I wish it was her own sight in a box, John."

"I wish it was, or could be!" cried the Carrier.

"Thank'ee," said the little man. "You speak very hearty. To think that she should never see the Dolls—and them a staring at her, so bold all day long! That's where it cuts. What's the damage, John?"

"I'll damage you," said John, "if you inquire. Dot! Very near?"

"Well! it's like you to say so," observed the little man. "It's your kind way. Let me see. I think that's all."

"I think not," said the Carrier. "Try again."

"Something for our Governor, eh?" said Caleb after pondering a little while. "To be sure. That's what I came for: but my head's so running on them Arks and things! He hasn't been here, has he?"

"Not he," returned the Carrier. "He's too busy, courting."

"He's coming round though," said Caleb; "for he told me to keep on the near side of the road going home, and it was ten to one he'd take me up. I had better go, by the bye—You couldn't have the goodness to let me pinch Boxer's tail, Mum, for half a moment could you?"

"Why, Caleb! what a question!"

"Oh never mind, Mum," said the little man. "He mightn't like it perhaps. There's a small order just come in, for barking dogs; and I should wish to go as close to Natur' as I could, for sixpence. That's all. Never mind Mum."

It happened opportunely, that Boxer, without receiving the proposed stimulus, began to bark with great zeal. But, as this implied the approach of some new visitor, Caleb, postponing his study from the life to a more convenient season, shouldered the round box, and took a hurried leave. He might have spared himself the trouble, for he met the visitor upon the threshold.

"Oh! You are here, are you? Wait a bit. I'll take you home. John Peerybingle, my service to you. More of my service to your pretty wife. Handsomer every day! Better too, if possible! And younger," mused the speaker, in a low voice; "that's the Devil of it!"

"I should be astonished at your paying compliments, Mr. Tackleton," said Dot, not with the best grace in the world; "but for your condition."

"You know all about it then?"

"I have got myself to believe it, somehow," said Dot.

"After a hard struggle, I suppose?"

"Very."

Tackleton the Toy-merchant, pretty generally known as Gruff and Tackleton—for that was the firm, though Gruff had been bought out long ago; only leaving his name, and as some said his nature, according to its Dictionary meaning, in the business. Cramped and chafing in the peaceable pursuit of toy-making, Tackleton was a domestic Ogre, who had been living on children all his life, and was their implacable enemy. He despised all toys; wouldn't have bought one for the world; delighted, in his malice, to insinuate grim expressions into the faces of brown paper farmers who drove pigs to market, bellmen who advertised lost lawyers' consciences, movable old ladies who darned stockings or carved pies; and other like samples of his stock in trade. In appalling masks; hideous, hairy, red-eyed Jacks in Boxes; Vampire Kites; Tumblers who wouldn't lie down and were perpetually flying forward, to stare infants out of countenance; his soul revelled. They were his only relief, and safety-valve. He was great in such inventions. Anything suggestive of a Pony-nightmare, was delicious to him. He had even lost money (and he took to that toy very kindly) by getting up Goblin slides for magic-lanterns, whereon the Powers of Darkness were depicted as a sort of supernatural shell-fish, with human faces. In intensifying the portraiture of Giants, he had sunk quite a little capital; and, though no painter himself, he could indicate, for the instruction of his artists, with a piece of chalk, a certain furtive leer for the countenances of those monsters, which was safe to destroy the peace of mind of any young gentleman between the ages of six and eleven, for the whole Christmas or Midsummer Vacation.

What he was in toys, he was (as most men are) in other things. You may easily suppose, therefore, that within the great green cape, which reached down to the calves of his legs, there was buttoned up to the chin an uncommonly pleasant fellow; and that he was about as choice a spirit, and as agreeable a companion, as ever stood in a pair of bull-headed looking boots with mahogany-colored tops.

He didn't look much like a bridegroom, as he stood in the Carrier's kitchen, with a twist in his dry face, and a screw in his body, and his hat jerked over the bridge of his nose, and his hands tucked down into the bottoms of his pockets, and his whole sarcastic ill-conditioned self peering out of one little corner of one little eye, like the concentrated essence of any number of ravens. But, a Bridegroom he designed to be.

"In three days' time. Next Thursday. The last day of the first month in the year. That's my wedding-day," said Tackleton.

Did I mention that he had always one eye wide open, and one eye nearly shut; and that the one eye nearly shut, was always the expressive eye? I don't think I did.

"That's my wedding-day!" said Tackleton, rattling his money.

"Why, it's our wedding-day too," exclaimed the Carrier.

"Ha ha!" laughed Tackleton. "Odd! You're just such another couple. Just!"

The indignation of Dot at this presumptuous assertion is not to be described. What next? His imagination would compass the possibility of just such another Baby, perhaps. The man was mad.

"I say! A word with you," murmured Tackleton, nudging the Carrier with his elbow, and taking him a little apart. "You'll come to the wedding? We're in the same boat, you know."

"How in the same boat?" inquired the Carrier.

"A little disparity, you know;" said Tackleton, with another nudge. "Come and spend an evening with us, beforehand."

"Why?" demanded John, astonished at this pressing hospitality.

"Why?" returned the other. "That's a new way of receiving an invitation. Why, for pleasure—sociability, you know, and all that!"

"I thought you were never sociable," said John, in his plain way.

"Tchah! It's of no use to be anything but free with you I see," said Tackleton. "Why, then, the truth is you have a—what tea-drinking people call a sort of comfortable appearance together, you and your wife. We know better, you know, but—"

"No, we don't know better," interposed John. "What are you talking about?"

"Well! We *don't* know better, then," said Tackleton. "We'll agree that we don't. As you like; what does it matter? I was going to say, as you have that sort of appearance, your company will produce a favorable effect on Mrs. Tackleton that will be. And, though I don't think your good lady's very friendly to me, in this matter, still she can't help herself from falling into my views, for there's a compactness and coziness of appearance about her that always tells, even in an indifferent case. You'll say you'll come?"

"We have arranged to keep our Wedding-Day (as far as that goes) at home," said John. "We have made the promise to ourselves these six months. We think, you see, that home—"

"Bah! what's home?" cried Tackleton. "Four walls and a ceiling! (why don't you kill that Cricket; *I* would! I always do. I hate their noise.) There are four walls and a ceiling at my house. Come to me!"

"You kill your Crickets, eh?" said John.

"Scrunch 'em, sir," returned the other, setting his heel heavily on the floor. "You'll say you'll come? It's as much your interest as mine, you know, that the women should persuade each other that they're quiet and contented, and couldn't be better off. I know their way. Whatever one woman says, another woman is determined to clinch, always. There's that spirit of emulation among 'em, sir, that if your wife says to my wife, 'I'm the happiest woman in the world, and mine's the best husband in the world, and I dote on him,' my wife will say the same to yours, or more, and half believe it."

"Do you mean to say she don't, then?" asked the Carrier.

"Don't!" cried Tackleton, with a short, sharp laugh. "Don't what?"

The Carrier had some faint idea of adding, "dote upon you." But, happening to meet the half-closed eye, as it twinkled upon him over the turned up collar of the cape, which was within an ace of poking it out, he felt it such an unlikely part and parcel of anything to be doted on, that he substituted, "that she don't believe it?"

"Ah you dog! You're joking," said Tackleton.

But the Carrier, though slow to understand the full drift of his meaning, eyed him in such a serious manner, that he was obliged to be a little more explanatory.

"I have the humor, sir, to marry a young wife, and a pretty wife:" here he rapped his little finger, to express the Bride; not sparingly, but sharply; with a sense of power. "I'm able to gratify that humor and I do. It's my whim. But—now look there!"

He pointed to where Dot was sitting, thoughtfully, before the fire; leaning her dimpled chin upon her hand, and watching the bright blaze.

"She honors and obeys, no doubt, you know," said Tackleton; "and that, as I am not a man of sentiment, is quite enough for *me*. But do you think there's anything more in it?"

"I think," observed the Carrier, "that I should chuck any man out of window, who said there wasn't."

"Exactly so," returned the other with an unusual alacrity of assent. "To be sure! Doubtless you would. Of course. I'm certain of it. Good-night. Pleasant dreams!"

The Carrier was puzzled, and made uncomfortable and uncertain, in spite of himself. He couldn't help showing it, in his manner.

"Good-night, my dear friend!" said Tackleton, compassionately. "I'm off. We're exactly alike, in reality, I see. You won't give us to-morrow evening? Well! Next day you go out visiting, I know. I'll meet you there, and bring my wife that is to be. It'll do her good. You're agreeable? Thank'ee. What's that!"

It was a loud cry from the Carrier's wife: a loud, sharp, sudden cry, that made the room ring, like a glass vessel. She had risen from her seat, and stood like one transfixed by terror and surprise. The Stranger had advanced towards the fire to warm himself, and stood within a short stride of her chair. But quite still.

"Dot!" cried the Carrier. "Mary! Darling! What's the matter? Are you ill! What is it? Tell me, dear!"

She only answered by beating her hands together, and falling into a wild fit of laughter. Then, sinking from his grasp upon the ground, she covered her face with her apron, and wept bitterly. And then she laughed again, and then she said how cold it was, and suffered him to lead her to the fire, where she sat down as before. The old man standing, as before, quite still.

"I'm better, John," she said. "I'm quite well now—I—"

"John!" But John was on the other side of her. Why turn her face towards the strange old gentleman, as if addressing him! Was her brain wandering?

"Only a fancy, John dear—a kind of shock—a something coming suddenly before my eyes—I don't know what it was. It's quite gone, quite gone."

"I'm glad it's gone," muttered Tackleton, turning the expressive eye all round the room. "I wonder where it's gone, and what it was. Humph! Caleb, come here! Who's that with the gray hair?"

"I don't know, sir," returned Caleb in a whisper. "Never see him before, in all my life. A beautiful figure for a nutcracker; quite a new model. With a screw-jaw opening down into his waistcoat, he'd be lovely."

"Not ugly enough," said Tackleton. "Nothing in him at all! Come! Bring that box! All right now, I hope?"

"Oh quite gone! Quite gone!" said the little woman, waving him hurriedly away. "Good-night!"

"Good-night," said Tackleton. "Good-night, John Peerybingle!"

So, with another sharp look round the room, he went out at the door; followed by Caleb with the wedding-cake on his head.

The Carrier had been so much astounded by his little wife, and so busily engaged in soothing and tending her, that he had scarcely been conscious of the Stranger's presence, until now, when he again stood there, their only guest.

"He don't belong to them, you see," said John. "I must give him a hint to go."

"I beg your pardon, friend," said the old gentleman, advancing to him; "the more so, as I fear your wife has not been well; but the Attendant whom my infirmity," he touched his ears and shook his head, "renders almost indispensable, not having arrived, I fear there must be some mistake. The bad night which made the shelter of your comfortable cart (may I never have a worse!) so acceptable, is still as bad as ever. Would you, in your kindness, suffer me to rent a bed here?"

"Yes, yes," cried Dot. "Yes! Certainly!"

"Oh!" said the Carrier, surprised by the rapidity of this consent. "Well! I don't object; but, still I'm not quite sure that—"

"Hush!" she interrupted. "Dear John!"

"Why, he's stone deaf," urged John.

"I know he is, but—Yes sir, certainly. Yes! certainly! I'll make him up a bed, directly, John."

As she hurried off to do it, the flutter of her spirits, and the agitation of her manner, were so strange, that the Carrier stood looking after her, quite confounded.

"Did its mothers make it up a Beds then!" cried Miss Slowboy to the Baby; "and did its hair grow brown and curly, when its caps was lifted off, and frighten it, a precious Pets, a-sitting by the fires!"

"And frighten it a precious Pets, a-sitting by the fires. What frightened Dot, I wonder!" mused the Carrier, pacing to and fro.

He scouted, from his heart, the insinuations of the Toy-merchant, and yet they filled him with a vague, indefinite uneasiness. For, Tackleton was quick and sly; and he had that painful sense, himself, of being a man of slow perception, that a broken hint was always worrying to him. He certainly had no intention in his mind of linking anything that Tackleton had said, with the unusual conduct of his wife, but the two subjects of reflection came into his mind together, and he could not keep them asunder.

The bed was soon made ready; and the visitor, declining all refreshment but a cup of tea, retired. Then, Dot—quite well again, she said, quite well again—arranged the great chair in the chimney-corner for her husband; filled his pipe and gave it him; and took her usual little stool beside him on the hearth.

She was, out and out, the very best filler of a pipe, I should say, in the four quarters of the globe. As to the tobacco, she was perfect mistress of the subject; and her lighting of the pipe was Art, high Art.

And the Cricket and the kettle, turning up again, acknowledged it! The bright fire, blazing again, acknowledged it! The little Mower on the clock, in his unheeded work, acknowledged it! The Carrier, in his smoothing forehead and expanding face, acknowledged it, the readiest of all.

And as he soberly and thoughtfully puffed at his old pipe, and as the Dutch clock ticked, and as the red fire gleamed, and as the Cricket chirped; that Genius of his Hearth and Home (for such the Cricket was) came out, in fairy shape, into the room, and summoned many forms of Home about him. Dots of all ages, and all sizes, filled the chamber. Dots who were merry children, running on before him gathering flowers, in the fields; coy Dots, half shrinking from, half yielding to, the pleading of his own rough image; newly-married Dots alighting at the door, and taking wondering possession of the household keys; motherly little Dots, attended by fictitious Slowboys, bearing babies to be christened; matronly Dots, still young and blooming, watching Dots of daughters, as they danced at rustic balls, fat Dots, encircled and beset by troops of rosy grandchildren; withered Dots, who leant on sticks, and tottered as they crept along. Old Carriers too, appeared, with blind Boxers lying at their feet; and sick Carriers, tended by the gentlest hands. And as the Cricket showed him all these things—he saw them plainly, though his eyes were fixed upon the fire—the Carrier's heart grew light and happy.

But what was that young figure of a man, which the same Fairy Cricket set so near Her stool, and which remained there, singly and alone? Why did it linger still, so near her, with its arms upon the chimney-piece, ever repeating "Married! and not to me!"

O Dot! O failing Dot! There is no place for it in all your husband's visions; why has its shadow fallen on his hearth!

🦗 Chirp the Second.

Caleb Plummer and his Blind Daughter lived all alone by themselves, in a little cracked nutshell of a wooden house, which was, in truth, no better than a pimple on the prominent red-brick nose of Gruff and Tackleton. The premises of Gruff and Tackleton were the great feature of the street; but you might have knocked down Caleb Plummer's dwelling with a hammer or two, and carried off the pieces in a cart.

I have said that Caleb and his poor Blind Daughter lived here. I should have said that Caleb lived here, and his poor Blind Daughter somewhere else—in an enchanted home of Caleb's furnishing, where scarcity and shabbiness were not, and trouble never entered. Caleb was no sorcerer, but in the only magic art that still remains to us, the magic of devoted, deathless love.

The Blind Girl never knew that ceilings were discolored, walls blotched and bare of plaster here and there, high crevices unstopped and widening every day, beams mouldering and tending downward. The Blind Girl never knew that iron was rusting, wood rotting, paper peeling off; the size, and shape, and true proportion of the dwelling, withering away. The Blind Girl never knew that ugly shapes of delf and earthenware were on the board; that sorrow and faintheartedness were in the house; that Caleb's scanty hairs were turning grayer and more gray, before her sightless face. The Blind Girl never knew they had a master, cold, exacting, and uninterested—never knew that Tackleton was Tackleton in short; but lived in the belief of an eccentric humorist who loved to have his jest with them, and who, while he was the Guardian Angel of their lives, disdained to hear one word of thankfulness.

And all was Caleb's doing; all the doing of her simple father! But he too had a Cricket on his Hearth; and listening sadly to its music when the motherless Blind Child was very young, that Spirit had inspired him with the thought that even her great deprivation might be almost changed into a blessing, and the girl made happy by these little means.

Caleb and his daughter were at work together in their usual working-room, which served them for their ordinary living-room as well; and a strange place it was. There were houses in it, finished and unfinished, for Dolls of all stations in life.

There were various other samples of his handicraft, besides Dolls, in Caleb Plummer's room. There were Noah's Arks, in which the Birds and Beasts were an uncommonly tight fit, I assure you; though they could be crammed in, anyhow, at the roof, and rattled and shaken into the smallest compass. By a bold poetical license, most of these Noah's Arks had knockers on the doors; inconsistent appendages, yet a pleasant finish to the outside of the building. There were scores of melancholy little carts which, when the wheels went round, performed most doleful music. Many small fiddles, drums, and other instruments of torture; no end of cannon, shields, swords, spears, and guns. There were beasts of all sorts: horses, in particular, of every breed, from the spotted barrel on four pegs, with a small tippet for a mane, to the thoroughbred rocker on his highest mettle. As it would have been hard to count the dozens of grotesque figures that were ever ready to commit all sorts of absurdities on the turning of a handle, so it would have been no easy task to mention any human folly, vice or weakness, that had not its type, immediate or remote, in Caleb Plummer's room. And not in an exaggerated form, for very little handles will move men and women to as strange performances, as any Toy was ever made to undertake.

In the midst of all these objects, Caleb and his daughter sat at work. The Blind Girl busy as a Doll's dressmaker; Caleb painting and glazing the four-pair front of a desirable family mansion.

"So you were out in the rain last night, father, in your beautiful new great-coat," said Caleb's daughter.

"In my beautiful new great-coat," answered Caleb, glancing towards a clothes-line in the room, on which the sack-cloth garment previously described, was carefully hung up to dry.

"How glad I am you bought it, father!"

"And of such a tailor, too," said Caleb. "Quite a fashionable tailor. It's too good for me."

The Blind Girl rested from her work, and laughed with delight. "Too good, father! What can be too good for you?"

"I'm half-ashamed to wear it though," said Caleb, watching the effect of what he said, upon her brightening face; "upon my word! When I hear the boys and people say behind me, 'Hal-loa! Here's a swell!' I don't know which way to look. And when the beggar wouldn't go away last night; and when I said I was a very common man, said 'No, your Honor! Bless your Honor, don't say that!' I was quite ashamed. I really felt as if I hadn't a right to wear it."

Happy Blind Girl! How merry she was in her exultation!

"I see you, father," she said, clasping her hands, "as plainly, as if I had the eyes I never want when you are with me. A blue coat"—

"Bright blue," said Caleb.

"Yes, yes! Bright blue!" exclaimed the girl, turning up her radiant face; "the color I can just remember in the blessed sky! You told me it was blue before! A bright blue coat"—

"Made loose to the figure," suggested Caleb.

"Made loose to the figure!" cried the Blind Girl, laughing heartily; "and in it, you, dear father, with your merry eye, your smiling face, your free step, and your dark hair—looking so young and handsome!"

"Halloa! Halloa!" said Caleb. "I shall be vain, presently!"

"I think you are, already," cried the Blind Girl, pointing at him, in her glee. "I know you, father! Ha, ha, ha! I've found you out, you see!"

"There we are," said Caleb, falling back a pace or two to form the better judgment of his work; "as near the real thing as sixpenn'orth of halfpence is to sixpence. What a pity that the whole front of the house opens at once! If there was only a staircase in it, now, and regular doors to the rooms to go in at! But that's the worst of my calling, I'm always deluding myself, and swindling myself."

"You are speaking quite softly. You are not tired, father?"

"Tired!" echoed Caleb, with a great burst of animation, "what should tire me, Bertha? *I* was never tired. What does it mean?"

To give the greater force to his words, he checked himself in an involuntary imitation of two half-length stretching and yawning figures on the mantel-shelf, who were represented as in one eternal state of weariness from the waist upwards; and hummed a fragment of a song. It was a Bacchanalian song, something about a Sparkling Bowl. He sang it with an assumption of a Devil-may-care voice, that made his face a thousand times more meagre and more thoughtful than ever.

"What! You're singing, are you?" said Tackleton, putting his head in at the door. "Go it! *I* can't sing."

Nobody would have suspected him of it. He hadn't what is generally termed a singing face, by any means.

"I can't afford to sing," said Tackleton. "I'm glad *you* can. I hope you can afford to work too. Hardly time for both, I should think?"

"If you could only see him, Bertha, how he's winking at me!" whispered Caleb. "Such a man to joke! you'd think, if you didn't know him, he was in earnest—wouldn't you now?"

The Blind Girl smiled and nodded.

"The bird that can sing and won't sing, must be made to sing, they say," grumbled Tackleton. "What about the owl that can't sing, and oughtn't to sing, and will sing; is there anything that *he* should be made to do?"

"The extent to which he's winking at this moment!" whispered Caleb to his daughter. "O, my gracious!"

"Always merry and lighthearted with us!" cried the smiling Bertha.

"O, you're there, are you?" answered Tackleton. "Poor Idiot!"

He really did believe she was an Idiot; and he founded the belief, I can't say whether consciously or not, upon her being fond of him.

"Well! and being there,—how are you?" said Tackleton, in his gruding way.

"Oh! well; quite well. And as happy as even you can wish me to be. As happy as you would make the whole world, if you could!"

The Blind Girl took his hand and kissed it; held it for a moment in her own two hands; and laid her cheek against it tenderly, before releasing it. There was such unspeakable affection and such fervent gratitude in the act, that Tackleton himself was moved.

"Bertha!" said Tackleton, assuming, for the nonce, a little cordiality. "Shall I tell you a secret, Bertha?"

"If you will!" she answered, eagerly.

How bright the darkened face! How adorned with light, the listening head!

"This is the day on which little what's-her-name, the spoilt child, Peerybingle's wife, pays her regular visit to you—makes her fantastic Pic-Nic here; ain't it?" said Tackleton, with a strong expression of distaste for the whole concern.

"Yes," replied Bertha. "This is the day."

"I thought so," said Tackleton. "I should like to join the party."

"Do you hear that, father!" cried the Blind Girl in an ecstasy.

"Yes, yes, I hear it," murmured Caleb, with the fixed look of a sleep-walker; "but I don't believe it. It's one of my lies, I've no doubt."

"You see I—I want to bring the Peerybingles a little more into company with May Fielding," said Tackleton. "I am going to be married to May."

"Married!" cried the Blind Girl, starting from him.

"She's such a con-founded Idiot," muttered Tackleton, "that I was afraid she'd never comprehend me. Ah, Bertha! Married! Church, parson, clerk, beadle, glass-coach, bells, breakfast, bride-cake, favors, marrow-bones, cleavers, and all the rest of the tom-foolery. A wedding, you know; a wedding. Don't you know what a wedding is?"

"I know," replied the Blind Girl, in a gentle tone. "I understand!"

"Do you?" muttered Tackleton. "It's more than I expected. Well! On that account I want to join the party, and to bring May and her mother. I'll send in a little something or other, before the afternoon. A cold leg of mutton, or some comfortable trifle of that sort. You'll expect me?"

"Yes," she answered.

She had drooped her head, and turned away: and so stood, with her hands crossed, musing.

"I don't think you will," muttered Tackleton, looking at her; "for you seem to have forgotten all about it already. Caleb!"

"I may venture to say I'm here, I suppose," thought Caleb. "Sir!"

"Take care she don't forget what I've been saying to her."

"*She* never forgets," returned Caleb. "It's one of the few things she an't clever in."

"Every man thinks his own geese swans," observed the Toy-merchant, with a shrug. "Poor devil!"

Having delivered himself of which remark, with infinite contempt, old Gruff and Tackleton withdrew.

Bertha remained where he had left her, lost in meditation. The gayety had vanished from her downcast face, and it was very sad. Three or four times, she shook her head, as if bewailing some remembrance or some loss; but, her sorrowful reflections found no vent in words.

It was not until Caleb had been occupied, some time, in yoking a team of horses to a wagon by the summary process of nailing the harness to the vital parts of their bodies, that she drew near to his working-stool, and sitting down beside him, said:

"Father, I am lonely in the dark. I want my eyes, my patient, willing eyes."

"Here they are," said Caleb. "Always ready. They are more yours than mine, Bertha, any hour in the four-and-twenty. What shall your eyes do for you, dear?"

"Look round the room, father."

"All right," said Caleb. "No sooner said than done, Bertha."

"Tell me about it."

"It's much the same as usual," said Caleb. "Homely, but very snug. The gay colors on the walls; the bright flowers on the plates and dishes; the shining wood, where there are beams or panels; the general cheerfulness and neatness of the building; make it very pretty.

"You have your working dress on, and are not so gallant as when you wear the handsome coat?" said Bertha, touching him.

"Not quite so gallant," answered Caleb. "Pretty brisk though."

"Father," said the Blind Girl, drawing close to his side, and stealing one arm round his neck, "tell me something about May. She is very fair?"

"She is indeed," said Caleb. And she was indeed. It was quite a rare thing to Caleb not to have to draw on his invention.

"Her hair is dark," said Bertha, pensively, "darker than mine. Her voice is sweet and musical, I know. I have often loved to hear it. Her shape—"

"There's not a Doll's in all the room to equal it," said Caleb. "And her eyes!"—

He stopped; for Bertha had drawn closer round his neck, and, from the arm that clung about him, came a warning pressure which he understood too well.

He coughed a moment, hammered for a moment, and then fell back upon the song about the sparkling bowl; his infallible resource in all such difficulties.

"Our friend, father, our benefactor. I am never tired you know of hearing about him.—Now, was I ever?" she said, hastily.

"Of course not," answered Caleb, "and with reason."

"Ah! With how much reason!" cried the Blind Girl, with such fervency, that Caleb, though his motives were so pure, could not endure to meet her face; but dropped his eyes, as if she could have read in them his innocent deceit.

"Then, tell me again about him, dear father," said Bertha. "Many times again! His face is benevolent, kind, and tender. Honest and true, I am sure it is. The manly heart that tries to cloak all favors with a show of roughness and unwillingness, beats in its every look and glance."

"And makes it noble," added Caleb, in his quiet desperation.

"And makes it noble!" cried the Blind Girl. "He is older than May, father."

"Ye-es," said Caleb, reluctantly. "He's a little older than May. But that don't signify."

"Oh father, yes! To be his patient companion in infirmity and age; to be his gentle nurse in sickness, and his constant friend in suffering and sorrow; to know no weariness in working for his sake; to watch him, tend him, sit beside his bed and talk to him awake, and pray for him asleep; what privileges these would be! What opportunities for proving all her truth and devotion to him! Would she do all this, dear father?"

"No doubt of it," said Caleb.

"I love her, father; I can love her from my soul!" exclaimed the Blind Girl. And saying so, she laid her poor blind face on Caleb's shoulder, and so wept and wept, that he was almost sorry to have brought that tearful happiness upon her.

In the mean time, there had been a pretty sharp commotion at John Peerybingle's, for, little Mrs. Peerybingle naturally couldn't think of going anywhere without the Baby; and to get the Baby under weigh, took time.

As to a chair, or anything of that kind for helping Mrs. Peerybingle into the cart, you know very little of John, if you think *that* was necessary. Before you could have seen him lift her from the ground, there she was in her place, fresh and rosy, saying, "John!"

"You've got the basket with the Veal and Ham-Pie and things, and the bottles of Beer?" said Dot. "If you haven't, you must turn round again, this very minute."

"You're a nice little article," returned the Carrier, "to be talking about turning round, after keeping me a full quarter of an hour behind my time."

"I am sorry for it, John," said Dot in a great bustle, "but I really could not think of going to Bertha's—I would not do it, John, on any account—without the Veal and Ham-Pie and things, and the bottles of Beer. Way!"

This monosyllable was addressed to the horse, who didn't mind it at all.

"Oh *do* way John!" said Mrs. Peerybingle. "Please!"

"It'll be time enough to do that," returned John, "when I begin to leave things behind me. The basket's here, safe enough."

"What a hard-hearted monster you must be, John, not to have said so, at once, and save me such a turn! I declared I wouldn't go to Bertha's without the Veal and Ham-Pie and things, for any money. Regularly once a fortnight ever since we have been married, John, have we made our little Pic-nic there. If anything was to go wrong with it, I should almost think we were never to be lucky again."

"By the bye—" observed the Carrier. "That old gentleman,"—

Again so visibly, and instantly embarrassed!

"He's an odd fish," said the Carrier, looking straight along the road before them. "I can't make him out. I don't believe there's any harm in him."

"None at all. I'm—I'm sure there's none at all."

"Yes," said the Carrier, with his eyes attracted to her face by the great earnestness of her manner. "I am glad you feel so certain of it, because it's a confirmation to me. It's curious that he should have taken in into his head to ask leave to go on lodging with us; an't it? Things come about so strangely."

"So very strangely," she rejoined in a low voice, scarcely audible.

"However, he's a good-natured old gentleman," said John, "and pays as a gentleman, and I think his word is to be relied upon, like a gentleman's. I had quite a long talk with him this morning: he can hear me better already, he says, as he gets more used to my voice. 'Why, I shall be returning home to-night your way,' he says, 'when I thought you'd be coming in an exactly opposite direction. That's capital! I may trouble you for another lift perhaps, but I'll engage not to fall so sound asleep again.' He *was* sound asleep, surely!— Dot! what are you thinking of?"

"Thinking of, John? I—I was listening to you."

"Oh! That's all right!" said the honest Carrier. "I was afraid, from the look of your face, that I had gone rambling on so as to set you thinking about something else."

Dot making no reply, they jogged on, for some little time, in silence.

The packages and parcels for the errand cart, were numerous; and there were many stoppages to take them in and give them out, which were not by any means the worst parts of the journey. Some people were so full of expectation about their parcels, and other people were so full of wonder about their parcels, and other people were so full of inexhaustible directions about their parcels, and John had such a lively interest in all the parcels, that it was as good as a play.

Of all these little incidents, Dot was the amused and open-eyed spectatress from her chair in the cart; and as she sat there, looking on—a charming little portrait framed to admiration by the tilt— there was no lack of nudgings and glancings and whisperings and envyings among the younger men. And this delighted John the Carrier, beyond measure; for he was proud to have his little wife admired, knowing that she didn't mind it—that, if anything, she rather liked it perhaps.

Boxer, who was in advance some quarter of a mile or so, had already passed the outposts of the town, and gained the corner of the street where Caleb and his daughter lived; and long before they had reached the door, he and the Blind Girl were on the pavement waiting to receive them.

May Fielding was already come; and so was her mother—a little querulous chip of an old lady with a peevish face. Gruff and Tackleton was also there, doing the agreeable, with the evident sensation of being as perfectly at home, and as unquestionably in his own element, as a fresh young salmon on the top of the Great Pyramid.

"May! My dear old friend!" cried Dot, running to meet her. "What a happiness to see you!"

Her old friend was, to the full, as hearty and as glad as she; and it really was, if you'll believe me, quite a pleasant sight to see them embrace. Tackleton was a man of taste, beyond all question. May was very pretty.

Tackleton led his intended mother-in-law to the post of honor. For the better gracing of this place at the high festival, the majestic old soul had adorned herself with a cap, calculated to inspire the thoughtless with sentiments of awe. She also wore her gloves. But let us be genteel, or die!

Caleb sat next his daughter; Dot and her old schoolfellow were side by side; the good Carrier took care of the bottom of the table. Miss Slowboy was isolated, for the time being, from every article of furniture but the chair she sat on, that she might have nothing to knock the Baby's head against.

As Tilly stared about her at the dolls and toys, they stared at her and at the company. The venerable old gentlemen at the street door (who were all in full action) showed especial interest in the party, pausing occasionally before leaping, as if they were listening to the conversation, and then plunging wildly over and over, a great many times, without halting for breath—as in a frantic state of delight with the whole proceedings.

"Ah May!" said Dot. "Dear dear, what changes! To talk of those merry school-days makes one young again."

"Why, you an't particularly old, at any time; are you?" said Tackleton.

"Look at my sober plodding husband there," returned Dot. "He adds twenty years to my age at least. Don't you, John?"

"Forty," John replied.

"How many *you'll* add to May's, I am sure, I don't know," said Dot, laughing. "But she can't be much less than a hundred years of age on her next birthday."

"Ha ha!" laughed Tackleton. Hollow as a drum, that laugh though. And he looked as if he could have twisted Dot's neck, comfortably.

"Dear, dear!" said Dot. "Only to remember how we used to talk, at school, about the husbands we would choose. I don't know how young, and how handsome, and how gay and how lively, mine was not to be! And as to May's!—Ah dear! I don't know whether to laugh or cry, when I think what silly girls we were."

May seemed to know which to do; for the color flushed into her face; and tears stood in her eyes.

"Even the very persons themselves—real live young men—were fixed on sometimes," said Dot. "We little thought how things would come about. I never fixed on John I'm sure; I never so much as thought of him. And if I had told you, you were ever to be married to Mr. Tackleton, why you'd have slapped me. Wouldn't you, May?"

Though May didn't say yes, she certainly didn't say no, or express no, by any means.

Tackleton laughed—quite shouted, he laughed so loud. John Peerybingle laughed too, in his ordinary good natured and contented manner; but his was a mere whisper of a laugh, to Tackleton's.

"You couldn't help yourselves, for all that. You couldn't resist us, you see," said Tackleton. "Here we are! Here we are! Where are your gay young bridegrooms now?"

"Some of them are dead," said Dot; "and some of them forgotten. Some of them, if they could stand among us at this moment, would not believe we were the same creatures; would not believe that what they saw and heard was real, and we *could* forget them so. No! they would not believe one word of it!"

"Why, Dot!" exclaimed the Carrier. "Little woman!"

She had spoken with such earnestness and fire, that she stood in need of some recalling to herself, without doubt. Her husband's check was very gentle, for he merely interfered, as he supposed, to shield old Tackleton; but it proved effectual, for she stopped, and said no more. There was an uncommon agitation, even in her silence, which the wary Tackleton, who had brought his half-shut eye to bear upon her, noted closely, and remembered to some purpose too.

In order that the bottled beer might not be slighted, John Peerybingle proposed To-morrow: the Wedding-Day; and called upon them to drink a bumper to it, before he proceeded on his journey.

There were two persons present, beside the bride and bridegroom elect, who did but indifferent honor to the toast. One of these was Dot, too flushed and discomposed to adapt herself to any small occurrence of the moment; the other, Bertha, who rose up hurriedly, before the rest, and left the table.

"Good-by!" said stout John Peerybingle, pulling on his dreadnought coat. "I shall be back at the old time. Good-by all!"

"Good-by John," returned Caleb.

He seemed to say it by rote, and to wave his hand in the same unconscious manner; for he stood observing Bertha with an anxious wondering face, that never altered its expression.

"Good-by young shaver!" said the jolly Carrier, bending down to kiss the child. Where's Dot?"

"I'm here John!" she said, starting.

"Come, come!" returned the Carrier, clapping his sounding hands. "Where's the pipe?"

"I quite forgot the pipe, John."

Forgot the pipe! Was such a wonder ever heard of! She! Forgot the pipe!

"I'll—I'll fill it directly. It's soon done."

But it was not so soon done, either. It lay in the usual place—the Carrier's dreadnought pocket—with the little pouch, her own work, from which she was used to fill it; but her hand shook so, that she entangled it (and yet her hand was small enough to have come out easily, I am sure), and bungled terribly. The filling of the pipe and lighting it, those little offices in which I have commended her discretion, were viley done, from first to last. During the whole process, Tackleton stood looking on maliciously with the half-closed eye; which, whenever it met hers—or caught it, for it can hardly be said to have ever met another eye: rather being a kind of trap to snatch it up—augmented her confusion in a most remarkable degree.

"Why, what a clumsy Dot you are, this afternoon!" said John. "I could have done it better myself, I verily believe!"

With these good-natured words, he strode away, and presently was heard, in company with Boxer, and the old horse, and the cart, making lively music down the road. What time the dreamy Caleb still stood, watching his blind daughter, with the same expression on his face.

"Bertha!" said Caleb, softly. "What has happened? How changed you are, my darling, in a few hours—since this morning. *You* silent and dull all day! What is it? Tell me!"

"Oh father, father!" cried the Blind Girl, bursting into tears. "Oh my hard, hard fate!"

Caleb drew his hand across his eyes before he answered her.

"But think how cheerful and how happy you have been, Bertha! How good, and how much loved, by many people."

"That strikes me to the heart, dear father! Always so mindful of me! Always so kind to me!"

Caleb was very much perplexed to understand her.

"To be—to be blind, Bertha, my poor dear," he faltered, "is a great affliction; but—"

"I have never felt it!" cried the Blind Girl. "I have never felt it, in its fulness. Never! I have sometimes wished that I could see you, or could see him—only once, dear father, only for one little minute—that I might know what it is I treasure up. I have wept in my prayers at night, to think that when your images ascended from my heart to Heaven, they might not be the true resemblance of yourselves. Oh my good, gentle father, bear with me, if I am wicked! This is not the sorrow that so weighs me down!"

Her father could not choose but let his moist eyes overflow; she was so earnest and pathetic, but he did not understand her, yet.

"Bring her to me," said Bertha. "I cannot hold it closed and shut within myself. Bring her to me, father!"

She knew he hesitated, and said, "May. Bring May!"

May heard the mention of her name, and coming quietly towards her, touched her on the arm. The Blind Girl turned immediately, and held her by both hands.

"Look into my face, Dear heart, Sweet heart!" said Bertha. "Read it with your beautiful eyes, and tell me if the truth is written on it."

"Dear Bertha, Yes!"

The Blind Girl addressed her in these words:

"There is not, in my soul, a wish or thought that is not for your good, bright May! There is not, in my soul, a grateful recollection stronger than the deep remembrance which is stored there, of the many many times when, in the full pride of sight and beauty, you have had consideration for Blind Bertha, even when we two were children, or when Bertha was as much a child as ever blindness can be! Every blessing on your head! Light upon your happy course! Not the less, my dear May, not the less, my bird, because, to-day, the knowledge that you are to be His wife has wrung my heart almost to breaking! Father, May, Mary! oh forgive me that it is so, for the sake of all he has done to relieve the weariness of my dark life: and for the sake of the belief you have in me, when I call Heaven to witness that I could not wish him married to a wife more worthy of his goodness!"

She dropped at last to the feet of her friend, and hid her blind face in the folds of her dress.

"Great Power!" exclaimed her father, smitten at one blow with the truth, "have I deceived her from the cradle, but to break her heart at last!"

Dot, recovering her self-possession, interposed, before May could reply, or Caleb say another word.

"Come come, dear Bertha! come away with me! Give her your arm, May. So! How composed she is, you see, already; and how good it is of her to mind us," said the cheery little woman, kissing her upon the forehead. "Come away, dear Bertha. Come! and here's her good father will come with her; wont you, Caleb? To—be—sure!"

Well, well! she was a noble little Dot in such things, and it must have been an obdurate nature that could have withstood her influence. When she had got poor Caleb and his Bertha away, that they might comfort and console each other, as she knew they only could, she presently came bouncing back to mount guard over that bridling little piece of consequence in the cap and gloves, and prevent the dear old creature from making discoveries.

"So bring me the precious Baby, Tilly," said she, drawing a chair to the fire; "and while I have it in my lap, here's Mrs. Fielding, Tilly, will tell me all about the management of Babies, and put me right in twenty points where I'm as wrong as can be. Won't you, Mrs. Fielding?"

Then, as it grew dark, and as it was a solemn part of this Institution of the Pic-Nic that Dot should perform all Bertha's household tasks, she trimmed the fire, and swept the hearth, and set the tea-board out, and drew the curtain, and lighted a candle. Then she played an air or two on a rude kind of harp, which Caleb had contrived for Bertha, and played them very well; for Nature had made her delicate little ear as choice a one for music as it would have been for jewels, if she had had any to wear. By this time it was the established hour for having tea.

Caleb and Bertha had returned some time before, and Caleb had set down to his afternoon's work. But he couldn't settle to it, poor fellow, being anxious and remorseful for his daughter.

When it was night, and tea was done, and Dot had nothing more to do in washing up the cups and saucers; in a word—for I must come toit and there is no use in putting it off—when the time drew nigh for expecting the Carrier's return in every sound of distant wheels, her manner changed again, her color came and went, and she was very restless.

Wheels heard. A horse's feet. The barking of a dog. The gradual approach of all the sounds. The scratching paw of Boxer at the door!

"Whose step is that!" cried Bertha, starting up.

"Whose step?" returned the Carrier, standing in the portal, with his brown face ruddy as a winter berry from the keen night air. "Why, mine."

"The other step," said Bertha. "The man's tread behind you!"

"She is not to be deceived," observed the Carrier, laughing. "Come along, sir. You'll be welcome, never fear!"

He spoke in a loud tone; and as he spoke, the deaf old gentleman entered.

"He's not so much a stranger, that you haven't seen him once, Caleb," said the Carrier. "You'll give him house-room till we go?"

"Oh surely John, and take it as an honor."

"He's the best company on earth, to talk secrets in," said John. "I have reasonable good lungs, but he tries 'em, I can tell you. Sit down sir. All friends here, and glad to see you!"

When he had imparted this assurance, in a voice that amply corroborated what he had said about his lungs, he added in his natural tone. "A chair in the chimney-corner, and leave to sit quite silent and look pleasantly about him, is all he cares for. He's easily pleased."

Bertha called Caleb to her side, when he had set the chair, and asked him, in a low voice, to describe their visitor.

The Carrier was in high spirits, good fellow that he was, and fonder of his little wife than ever.

"A clumsy Dot she was, this afternoon!" he said, encircling her with his rough arm, as she stood, removed from the rest; "and yet I like her somehow. See yonder, Dot!"

He pointed to the old man. She looked down. I think she trembled.

"He-s—ha ha ha!—he's full of admiration for you!" said the Carrier. "Talked of nothing else, the whole way here. Why, he's a brave old boy. I like him for it!"

"I wish he had had a better subject, John;" she said, with an uneasy glance about the room. At Tackleton especially.

"A better subject!" cried the jovial John. "There's no such thing. Come, off with the great-coat, off with the thick shawl, off with the heavy wrappers! and a cosy half-hour by the fire! My humble service, Mistress. A game at cribbage, you and I? That's hearty!"

His challenge was addressed to the old lady, who accepting it with gracious readiness, they were soon engaged upon the game.

Thus, his whole attention gradually became absorbed upon the cards; and he thought of nothing else, until a hand upon his shoulder restored him to a consciousness of Tackleton.

"I am sorry to disturb you—but a word, directly."

"I'm going to deal," returned the Carrier. "It's a crisis."

"It is," said Tackleton. "Come here, man!"

"What is it?" asked the Carrier, with a frightened aspect.

"Hush! I'll show you, if you'll come with me."

The Carrier accompanied him, without another word. They went across a yard, where the stars were shining, and by a little side-door, into Tackleton's own counting-house, where there was a glass window commanding the ware-room, which was closed for the night. There was no light in the counting-house itself, but there were lamps in the long narrow ware-room; and consequently the window was bright.

"A moment!" said Tackleton. "Can you bear to look through that window, do you think?"

"Why not?" returned the Carrier.

"A moment more," said Tackleton. "Don't commit any violence. It's of no use. It's dangerous too. You're a strong-made man; and you might do murder before you know it."

In one stride he was at the window, and he saw—

Oh Shadow on the Hearth! O truthful Cricket! Oh perfidious wife!

He saw her, with the old man—old no longer, but erect and gallant—bearing in his hand the false white hair that had won his way into their desolate and miserable home. He saw her listening to him, as he bent his head to whisper in her ear; and suffering him to clasp her round the waist, as they moved slowly down the long wooden gallery towards the door by which they had entered it. He saw them stop, and saw her turn—to have the face, the face he loved so, so presented to his view!—and saw her, with her own hands, adjust the lie upon his head, laughing, as she did it, at his unsuspicious nature!

He clenched his strong right-hand at first, as if he would have beaten down a lion. But opening it immediately again, he spread it out before the eyes of Tackleton (for he was tender of her, even then), and so, as they passed out, fell down upon a desk, and was as weak as any infant.

He was wrapped up to the chin, and busy with his horse and parcels, when she came into the room, prepared for going home.

"Now John, dear! Good-night May! Good-night Bertha!"

Could she kiss them? Could she be blithe and cheerful in her parting? Could she venture to reveal her face to them without a blush? Yes. Tackleton observed her closely, and she did all this.

Tilly was hushing the Baby, and she crossed and re-crossed Tackleton, a dozen times, repeating drowsily:

"Did the knowledge that it was to be its wifes, then, wring its hearts almost to breaking; and did its fathers deceive it from its cradles but to break its hearts at last!"

"Now Tilly, give me the Baby! Good-night, Mr. Tackleton. Where's John, for goodness' sake?"

"He's going to walk, beside the horse's head," said Tackleton; who helped her to her seat.

"My dear John. Walk? To-night?"

The muffled figure of her husband made a hasty sign in the affirmative; and the false stranger and the little nurse being in their places, the old horse moved off.

When Tackleton had gone off likewise, escorting May and her mother home, poor Caleb sat down by the fire beside his daughter; anxious and remorseful at the core; and still saying in his wistful contemplation of her, "Have I deceived her from the cradle, but to break her heart at last!"

🐾 Chirp the Third.

The Dutch clock in the corner struck Ten, when the Carrier sat down by his fireside. So troubled and grief-worn, that he seemed to scare the Cuckoo, who, having cut his ten melodious announcements as short as possible, plunged back into the Moorish Palace again, and clapped his little door behind him, as if the unwonted spectacle were too much for his feelings.

If the little Haymaker had been armed with the sharpest of scythes, and had cut at every stroke into the Carrier's heart, he never could have gashed and wounded it, as Dot had done.

It was a heart so full of love for her; so bound up and held together by innumerable threads of winning remembrance, spun from the daily workings of her many qualities of endearments; it was a heart so single and so earnest in its Truth, so strong in right, so weak in wrong; that it could cherish neither passion nor revenge at first, and had only room to hold the broken image of its Idol.

But, slowly, slowly, as the Carrier sat brooding on his hearth, now cold and dark, other and fiercer thoughts began to rise within him, as an angry wind comes rising in the night. The Stranger was beneath his outraged roof. Three steps would take him to his chamber-door. One blow would beat it in. "You might do murder before you know it," Tackleton had said. How could it be murder, if he gave the villain time to grapple with him hand to hand! He was the younger man.

He was the younger man! Yes, yes; some lover who had won the heart that *he* had never touched. Some lover of her early choice, of whom she had thought and dreamed, for whom she had pined and pined, when he had fancied her so happy by his side. O agony to think of it!

She had been above stairs with the Baby, getting it to bed. As he sat brooding on the hearth, she came close beside him, without his knowledge—in the turning of the rack of his great misery, he lost all other sounds—and put her little stool at his feet. He only knew it, when he felt her hand upon his own, and saw her looking up into his face.

With wonder? No. It was his first impression, and he was fain to look at her again, to set it right. No, not with wonder. With an eager and inquiring look; but not with wonder. At first it was alarmed and serious; then, it changed into a strange, wild, dreadful smile of recognition of his thoughts; then, there was nothing but her clasped hands on her brow, and her bent head, and falling hair.

Though the power of Omnipotence had been his to wield at that moment, he had too much of its diviner property of Mercy in his breast to have turned one feather's weight of it against her. But he could not bear to see her crouching down upon the little seat where he had often looked on her, with love and pride, so innocent and gay; and, when she rose and left him, sobbing as she went, he felt it a relief to have the vacant place beside him rather than her so long cherished presence. This in itself was anguish keener than all, reminding him how desolate he was become, and how the great bond of his life was rent asunder.

The more he felt this, the stronger rose his wrath against his enemy. He looked about him for a weapon.

There was a gun, hanging on the wall. He took it down, and moved a pace or two towards the door of the perfidious Stranger's room. Some shadowy idea that it was just to shoot this man like a wild beast, seized him, and dilated in his mind until it grew into a monstrous demon in complete possession of him, casting out all milder thoughts and setting up its undivided empire.

The phrase is wrong. Not casting out his milder thoughts, but artfully transforming them. Turning water into blood, love into hate, gentleness into blind ferocity. Her image, sorrowing, humbled, but still pleading to his tenderness and mercy with resistless power, never left his mind; but, staying there, it urged him to the door; raised the weapon to his shoulder; fitted and nerved his finger to the trigger; and cried "Kill him! In his bed!"

He reversed the gun to beat the stock upon the door; he already held it lifted in the air; some indistinct design was in his thoughts of calling out to him to fly, for God's sake, by the window—

When, suddenly, the struggling fire illumined the whole chimney with a glow of light; and the Cricket on the Hearth began to Chirp!

No sound he could have heard, no human voice, not even hers, could so have moved and softened him. The artless words in which she had told him of her love for this same Cricket, were once more freshly spoken; her trembling, earnest manner at the moment, was again before him; her pleasant voice—O what a voice it was, for making household music at the fireside of an honest man!—thrilled through and through his better nature, and awoke it into life and action.

He recoiled from the door, like a man walking in his sleep, awakened from a frightful dream: and put the gun aside. Clasping his hands before his face, he then sat down again beside the fire, and found relief in tears.

The Cricket on the Hearth came out into the room, and stood in Fairy shape before him.

" 'I love it,' " said the Fairy Voice, repeating what he well remembered, " 'for the many times I have heard it, and the many thoughts its harmless music has given me.' "

"She said so!" cried the Carrier. "True!"

" 'This has been a happy home, John: and I love the Cricket for its sake!' "

"It has been, Heaven knows," returned the Carrier. "She made it happy, always,—until now."

"So gracefully sweet-tempered; so domestic, joyful, busy, and light-hearted!" said the Voice.

"Otherwise I never could have loved her as I did," returned the Carrier.

The Voice, correcting him, said "do."

The Carrier repeated "as I did." But not firmly. His faltering tongue resisted his control, and would speak in its own way, for itself and him.

The Figure in an attitude of invocation, raised its head and said:

"Upon your own hearth"—

"The hearth she has blighted," interposed the Carrier.

"The hearth she has—how often!—blessed and brightened," said the Cricket; "the hearth which, but for her, were only a few stones and bricks and rusty bars, but which has been, through her, the Altar of your Home; on which you have nightly sacrificed some petty passion, selfishness, or care, and offered up the homage of a tranquil mind, a trusting nature, and an overflowing heart; so that the smoke from this poor chimney has gone upward with a better fragrance than the richest incense that is burnt before the richest shrines in all the gaudy temples of this world!—Upon your own hearth; in its quiet sanctuary; surrounded by its gentle influences and associations; hear her! Hear me! Hear everything that speaks the language of your hearth and home!"

"And pleads for her?" inquired the Carrier.

"All things that speak the language of your hearth and home, *must* plead for her!" returned the Cricket. "For they speak the truth."

And while the Carrier, with his head upon his hands, continued to sit meditating in his chair, the Presence stood beside him, suggesting his reflections by its power, and presenting them before him, as in a glass or picture. It was not a solitary Presence. From the hearthstone, from the chimney, from the clock, the pipe, the kettle, and the cradle; from the floor, the walls, the ceiling, and the stairs: from the cart without, and the cupboard within; from everything and every place with which she had ever been familiar, and with which she had ever entwined one recollection of herself in her unhappy husband's mind; Fairies came trooping forth. Not to stand beside him as the Cricket did, but to busy and bestir themselves. To do all honor to her image. To pull him by the skirts, and point to it when it appeared. To cluster round it, and embrace it, and strew flowers for it to tread on. To try to crown its fair head with their tiny hands. To show that they were fond of it and loved it; and that there was not one ugly, wicked, or accusatory creature to claim knowledge of it—none but their playful and approving selves.

His thoughts were constant to her image. It was always there.

She sat plying her needle, before the fire, and singing to herself. Such a blithe, thriving, steady little Dot! The fairy figures turned upon him all at once, by one consent, with one prodigious concentrated stare, and seemed to say "Is this the light wife you are mourning for!"

The staring figures turned upon him, and seemed to say "Is this the wife who has forsaken you!"

A shadow fell upon the mirror or the picture; call it what you will. A great shadow of the Stranger, as he first stood underneath their roof; covering its surface, and blotting out all other objects. But the nimble Fairies worked like bees to clear it off again. And Dot again was there. Still bright and beautiful.

Rocking her little Baby in its cradle, singing to it softly, and resting her head upon a shoulder which had its counterpart in the musing figure by which the Fairy Cricket stood.

The night—I mean the real night: not going by Fairy clocks— was wearing now; and in this stage of the Carrier's thoughts, the moon burst out, and shone brightly in the sky. Perhaps some calm and quiet light had risen also, in his mind; and he could think more soberly of what had happened.

Although the shadow of the Stranger fell at intervals upon the glass—always distinct, and big, and thoroughly defined—it never fell so darkly as at first. Whenever it appeared, the Fairies uttered a general cry of consternation, and plied their little arms and legs, with inconceivable activity, to rub it out. And whenever they got at Dot again, and showed her to him once more, bright and beautiful, they cheered in the most inspiring manner.

They never showed her, otherwise than beautiful and bright, they to whom falsehood is annihilation; and being so, what Dot was there for them, but the one active, beaming, pleasant little creature who had been the light and sun of the Carrier's Home!

The Fairies were prodigiously excited when they showed her, with the Baby, gossiping among a knot of sage old matrons, and affecting to be wondrous old and matronly herself, and leaning in a staid, demure old way upon her husband's arm, attempting—she! such a bud of a little woman—to convey the idea of having abjured the vanities of the world in general, and of being the sort of person to whom it was no novelty at all to be a mother; yet in the same breath, they showed her, laughing at the Carrier for being awkward, and pulling up his shirt-collar to make him smart, and mincing merrily about that very room to teach him how to dance!

They turned, and stared immensely at him when they showed her with the Blind Girl; for, though she carried cheerfulness and animation with her wheresoever she went, she bore those influences into Caleb Plummer's home, heaped up and running over. The Blind Girl's love for her, and trust in her, and gratitude to her; her own good busy way of setting Bertha's thanks aside; her dexterous little arts for filling up each moment of the visit in doing something useful to the house, and really working hard while feigning to make holiday; her radiant little face arriving at the door, and taking leave; the wonderful expression in her whole self, from her neat foot to the crown of her head, of being a part of the establishment—a something necessary to it, and loved her for. And once again they looked upon him all at once, appealingly, and seemed to say, while some among them nestled in her dress and fondled her, "Is this the wife who has betrayed your confidence!"

More than once, or twice, or thrice, in the long thoughtful night, they showed her to him sitting on her favorite seat, with her bent head, her hands clasped on her brow, her falling hair. As he had seen her last. And when they found her thus, they neither turned nor looked upon him, but gathered close round her, and comforted and kissed her, and pressed on one another to show sympathy and kindness to her, and forgot him altogether.

Thus the night passed. The moon went down; the stars grew pale; the cold day broke; the sun rose. The Carrier still sat, musing, in the chimney corner. He had sat there, with his head upon his hands, all night. All night the faithful Cricket had been Chirp, Chirp, Chirping on the Hearth. All night he had listened to its voice. All night the household Fairies had been busy with him. All night she had been amiable and blameless in the glass, except when that one shadow fell upon it.

He rose up when it was broad day, and washed and dressed himself. He couldn't go about his customary cheerful avocations— he wanted spirit for them—but it mattered the less, that it was

Tackleton's wedding-day, and he had arranged to make his rounds by proxy. He thought to have gone merrily to church with Dot. But such plans were at an end. It was their own wedding-day too. Ah! how little he had looked for such a close to such a year!

The Carrier had expected that Tackleton would pay him an early visit; and he was right. He had not walked to and fro before his own door, many minutes, when he saw the Toy-merchant coming in his chaise along the road. As the chaise drew nearer, he perceived that Tackleton was dressed out sprucely for his marriage, and that he had decorated his horse's head with flowers and favors.

"John Peerybingle!" said Tackleton, with an air of condolence. "My good fellow, how do you find yourself this morning?"

"I have had but a poor night, Master Tackleton," returned the Carrier shaking his head: "for I have been a good deal disturbed in my mind. But it's over now! Can you spare me half an hour or so, for some private talk?"

"I came on purpose," returned Tackleton, alighting. "Never mind the horse. He'll stand quiet enough, with the reins over this post, if you'll give him a mouthful of hay."

The Carrier having brought it from his stable, and set it before him, they turned into the house.

"You are not married before noon?" he said, "I think?"

"No," answered Tackleton. "Plenty of time. Plenty of time."

When they entered the kitchen, Tilly Slowboy was rapping at the Stranger's door; which was only removed from it by a few steps. One of her very red eyes (for Tilly had been crying all night long, because her mistress cried) was at the keyhole; and she was knocking very loud; and seemed frightened.

"If you please I can't make nobody hear," said Tilly, looking round. "I hope nobody an't gone and been and died if you please!"

This philanthropic wish, Miss Slowboy emphasized with various new raps and kicks at the door; which led to no result whatever.

"Shall I go?" said Tackleton. "It's curious."

The Carrier who had turned his face from the door, signed to him to go if he would.

So Tackleton went to Tilly Slowboy's relief; and he too kicked and knocked; and he too failed to get the least reply. But he thought of trying the handle of the door; and as it opened easily, he peeped in, looked in, went in, and soon came running out again.

"John Peerybingle," said Tackleton, in his ear. "I hope there has been nothing—nothing rash in the night?"

The Carrier turned upon him quickly.

"Because he's gone!" said Tackleton; "and the window's open. I don't see any marks—to be sure it's almost on a level with the garden: but I was afraid there might have been some—some scuffle. Eh?"

"Make yourself easy," said the Carrier. "He went into that room last night, without harm in word or deed from me, and no one has entered it since. He is away of his own free will. I'd go out gladly at that door, and beg my bread from house to house, for life, if I could so change the past that he had never come. But he has come and gone. And I have done with him!"

"Oh!—Well, I think he has got off pretty easy," said Tackleton, taking a chair.

The sneer was lost upon the Carrier, who sat down too, and shaded his face with his hand, for some little time, before proceeding.

"You showed me last night," he said at length, "my wife; my wife that I love; secretly—"

"And tenderly," insinuated Tackleton.

"Conniving at that man's disguise, and giving him opportunities of meeting her alone. I think there's no sight I wouldn't have rather seen than that. I think there's no man in the world I wouldn't have rather had to show it me."

"I confess to having had my suspicions always," said Tackleton. "And that has made me objectionable here I know."

"But as you did show it me," pursued the Carrier, not minding him; "and as you saw her, my wife, my wife that I love"—his voice, and eye, and hand, grew steadier and firmer as he repeated these words: evidently in pursuance of a steadfast purpose—"as you saw her at this disadvantage, it is right and just that you should also see with my eyes, and look into my breast, and know what my mind is, upon the subject. For it's settled," said the Carrier, regarding him attentively. "And nothing can shake it now."

Tackleton muttered a few general words of assent, about its being necessary to vindicate something or other; but he was overawed by the manner of his companion. Plain and unpolished as it was, it had a something dignified and noble in it, which nothing but the soul of generous honor dwelling in the man could have imparted.

"I am a plain, rough man," pursued the Carrier, "with very little to recommend me. I am not a clever man, as you very well know. I am not a young man. I love my little Dot, because I had seen her grow up, from a child, in her father's house; because I knew how precious she was; because she had been my life, for years and years. There's many men I can't compare with, who never could have loved my little Dot like me, I think!"

He paused, and softly beat the ground a short time with his foot, before resuming.

"I often thought that though I wasn't good enough for her, I should make her a kind husband, and perhaps know her value better than another; and in this way I reconciled it to myself, and came to think it might be possible that we should be married. And in the end it came about, and we *were* married."

"Hah!" said Tackleton, with a significant shake of the head.

"I had studied myself; I had had experience of myself; I knew how much I loved her, and how happy I should be," pursued the Carrier. "But I had not—I feel it now—sufficiently considered her."

"To be sure," said Tackleton. "Giddiness, frivolity, fickleness, love of admiration! Not considered! All left out of sight! Hah!"

"You had best not interrupt me," said the Carrier, with some sternness, "till you understand me; and you're wide of doing so!"

The Toy-merchant gazed at him in astonishment. He went on in a softer tone:

"Did I consider," said the Carrier, "that I took her—at her age, and with her beauty—from her young companions, and the many scenes of which she was the ornament, in which she was the brightest little star that ever shown, to shut her up from day to day in my dull house, and keep my tedious company? Did I consider how little suited I was to her sprightly humor, and how wearisome a plodding man like me must be, to one of her quick spirit? Never. I took advantage of her hopeful nature and her cheerful disposition; and I married her. I wish I never had! For her sake; not for mine!"

The Toy-merchant gazed at him, without winking. Even the half-shut eye was open now.

"Heaven bless her!" said the Carrier, "for the cheerful constancy with which she tried to keep the knowledge of this from me! And Heaven help me, that, in my slow mind, I have not found it out before! Poor child! Poor Dot! *I* not to find it out, who have seen her eyes fill with tears, when such a marriage as our own was spoken of! I, who have seen the secret trembling on her lips a hundred times, and never suspected it till last night! Poor girl! That I could ever hope she would be fond of me! That I could ever believe she was!"

"She made a show of it," said Tackleton. "She made such a show of it, that to tell you the truth it was the origin of my misgivings."

And here he asserted the superiority of May Fielding, who certainly made no sort of show of being fond of *him*.

"She has tried," said the poor Carrier, with greater emotion than he had exhibited yet; "I only now begin to know how hard she has tried, to be my dutiful and zealous wife. It will be some help and comfort to me, when I am here alone."

"Here alone?" said Tackleton. "Oh! Then you do mean to take some notice of this?"

"I mean," returned the Carrier, "to do her the greatest kindness, and make her the best reparation, in my power. I can release her from the daily pain of an unequal marriage, and the struggle to conceal it. She shall be as free as I can render her."

"Make *her* reparation!" exclaimed Tackleton, twisting and turning his great ears with his hands. "There must be something wrong here. You didn't say that, of course."

The Carrier set his grip upon the collar of the Toy-merchant, and shook him like a reed.

"Listen to me!" he said. "And take care that you hear me right. Listen to me. Do I speak plainly?"

"Very plainly indeed," answered Tackleton.

"As if I meant it?"

"Very much as if you meant it."

"I sat upon that hearth, last night, all night," exclaimed the Carrier. "On the spot where she has often sat beside me, with her sweet face looking into mine. I called up her whole life, day by day. I had her dear self, in its every passage, in review before me. And upon my soul she is innocent, if there is One to judge the innocent and guilty!"

Staunch Cricket on the Hearth! Loyal household Fairies!

"Passion and distrust have left me!" said the Carrier; "and nothing but my grief remains. In an unhappy moment some old lover, better suited to her tastes and years than I; forsaken, perhaps, for me, against her will; returned. In an unhappy moment, taken by surprise, and wanting time to think of what she did, she made herself a party to his treachery, by concealing it. Last night she saw him, in the interview we witnessed. It was wrong. But otherwise than this she is innocent if there is truth on earth!"

"If that is your opinion"—Tackleton began.

"So, let her go!" pursued the Carrier. "Go, with my blessing for the many happy hours she has given me, and my forgiveness for any pang she has caused me. Let her go, and have the peace of mind I wish her! Now, it's over!"

"O no, John, not over. Do not say it's over yet! Not quite yet. I have heard your noble words. I could not steal away, pretending to be ignorant of what has affected me with such deep gratitude. Do not say it's over, 'till the clock has struck again!"

She had entered shortly after Tackleton, and had remained there. She never looked at Tackleton, but fixed her eyes upon her husband. But she kept away from him, setting as wide a space as possible between them; and though she spoke with most impassioned earnestness, she went no nearer to him even then. How different in this from her old self!

"No hand can make the clock which will strike again for me the hours that are gone," replied the Carrier, with a faint smile. "But let it be so, if you will, my dear. It will strike soon. It's of little matter what we say. I'd try to please you in a harder case than that."

"Well!" muttered Tackleton. "I must be off, for when the clock strikes again, it'll be necessary for me to be upon my way to church. Good-morning, John Peerybingle. I'm sorry to be deprived of the pleasure of your company. Sorry for the loss, and the occasion of it too!"

"I have spoken plainly?" said the Carrier, accompanying him to the door.

"Oh quite!"

"And you'll remember what I have said?"

"Why, if you compel me to make the observation," said Tackleton, previously taking the precaution of getting into his chaise; "I must say that it was so very unexpected, that I'm far from being likely to forget it."

"The better for us both," returned the Carrier. "Good-by. I give you joy!"

"I wish I could give it to *you*," said Tackleton. "As I can't; thank'ee. Between ourselves, (as I told you before, eh?) I don't much think I shall have the less joy in my married life, because May hasn't been too officious about me, and too demonstrative. Good-by! Take care of yourself."

The Carrier stood looking after him until he was smaller in the distance than his horse's flowers and favors near at hand; and then, with a deep sigh, went strolling like a restless, broken man, among some neighboring elms; unwilling to return until the clock was on the eve of striking.

His little wife, being left alone, sobbed piteously; but often dried her eyes and checked herself, to say how good he was, how excellent he was! and once or twice she laughed; so heartily, triumphantly, and incoherently (still crying all the time), that Tilly was quite horrified.

"Will you bring him sometimes, to see his father, Tilly," inquired her mistress, drying her eyes; "when I can't live here, and have gone to my old home?"

The soft-hearted Slowboy trailed off at this juncture, into such a deplorable howl, the more tremendous from its long suppression, that she must infallibly have awakened the Baby, and frightened him into something serious (probably convulsions), if her eyes had not encountered Caleb Plummer, leading in his daughter. This spectacle restoring her to a sense of the proprieties, she stood for some few moments silent, with her mouth wide open; and then, posting off to the bed on which the Baby lay asleep, danced in a weird, Saint Vitus manner on the floor, and at the same time rummaged with her face and head among the bedclothes, apparently deriving much relief from those extraordinary operations.

"Mary!" said Bertha. "Not at the marriage!"

"I told her you would not be there mum," whispered Caleb. "I heard as much last night. But bless you," said the little man, taking her tenderly by both hands. *I* don't care for what they say. *I* don't believe them. There an't much of me, but that little should be torn to pieces sooner than I'd trust a word against you!"

He put his arms about her and hugged her, as a child might have hugged one of his own dolls.

"Bertha couldn't stay at home this morning," said Caleb. "She was afraid, I know, to hear the bells ring, and couldn't trust herself to be so near them on their wedding-day. So we started in good time, and came here. I have been thinking of what I have done," said Caleb, after a moment's pause; "I have been blaming myself till I hardly knew what to do or where to turn, for the distress of mind I have caused her; and I've come to the conclusion that I'd better, if you'll stay with me, mum, the while, tell her the truth. You'll stay with me the while?" he inquired, trembling from head to foot.

"Mary," said Bertha, "where is your hand! Ah! Here it is: here it is!" pressing it to her lips, with a smile, and drawing it through her arm. "I heard them speaking softly among themselves, last night, of some blame against you. They were wrong."

The Carrier's Wife was silent. Caleb answered for her.

"They were wrong," he said.

"I knew it!" cried Bertha, proudly. "I told them so. I scorned to hear a word! Blame *her* with justice!" she pressed her hand between her own, and the soft cheek against her face. "No! I am not so blind as that."

Her father went on one side of her, while Dot remained upon the other: holding her hand.

"I know you all," said Bertha, "better than you think. But none so well as her. Not even you, father. There is nothing half so real and so true about me, as she is. If I could be restored to sight this instant, and not a word were spoken, I could choose her from a crowd! My sister!"

"Bertha, my dear," said Caleb, "I have something on my mind I want to tell you, while we three are alone. Hear me kindly! I have a confession to make to you, my darling."

"A confession, father?"

"I have wandered from the truth and lost myself, my child," said Caleb, with a pitiable expression in his bewildered face. "I have wandered from the truth, intending to be kind to you; and have been cruel."

She turned her wonder-stricken face towards him, and repeated "Cruel!"

"He accuses himself too strongly, Bertha," said Dot. "You'll say so, presently. You'll be the first to tell him so."

"He cruel to me!" cried Bertha, with a smile of incredulity.

"Not meaning it, my child," said Caleb. "But I have been; though I never suspected it, till yesterday. My dear blind daughter, hear me and forgive me! The world you live in, heart of mine, doesn't exist as I have represented it. The eyes you trusted in, have been false to you."

She turned her wonder-stricken face towards him still; but drew back, and clung closer to her friend.

"Your road in life was rough, my poor one," said Caleb, "and I meant to smooth it for you. I have altered objects, changed the characters of people, invented many things that never have been, to make you happier. I have had concealments from you, put deceptions on you, God forgive me! and surrounded you with fancies."

"But living people are not fancies!" she said hurriedly, and turning very pale, and still retiring from him. "You can't change them."

"I have done so, Bertha," pleaded Caleb. "There is one person that you know, my dove—"

"Oh, father! why do you say I know!" she answered, in a tone of keen reproach. "What and whom do I know! I, who have no leader! I, so miserably blind!"

In the anguish of her heart, she stretched out her hands, as if she were groping her way; then spread them, in a manner most forlorn and sad, upon her face.

"The marriage that takes place to-day," said Caleb, "is with a stern, sordid, grinding man. A hard master to you and me, my dear, for many years. Ugly in his looks, and in his nature. Cold and callous always. Unlike what I have painted him to you in everything, my child. In everything."

"Oh, why," cried the Blind Girl, tortured, as it seemed, almost beyond endurance, "why did you ever do this! Why did you ever fill my heart so full, and then come in like Death, and tear away the objects of my love! O Heaven, how blind I am! How helpless and alone!"

Her afflicted father hung his head, and offered no reply but in his penitence and sorrow.

She had been but a short time in this passion of regret, when the Cricket on the Hearth, unheard by all but her, began to chirp. Not merrily, but in a low, faint sorrowing way. It was so mournful that her tears began to flow; and when the Presence which had been beside the Carrier all night, appeared behind her, pointing to her father, they fell down like rain.

She heard the Cricket-voice more plainly soon, and was conscious, through her blindness, of the Presence hovering about her father.

"Mary," said the Blind Girl, "tell me what my home is. What it truly is."

"It is a poor place, Bertha; very poor and bare indeed. The house will scarcely keep out wind and rain another winter. It is as roughly shielded from the weather, Bertha," Dot continued in a low, clear voice, "as your poor father in his sack-cloth coat."

The Blind Girl, greatly agitated, rose, and led the Carrier's little wife aside.

"Those presents that I took such care of; that came almost at my wish, and were so dearly welcome to me," she said, trembling; "where did they come from? Did you send them?"

"No."

"Who then?"

Dot saw she knew, already, and was silent. The Blind Girl spread her hands before her face again. But in quite another manner now.

"Dear Mary, a moment. One moment? More this way. Speak softly to me. You are true, I know. You'd not deceive me now; would you?"

"No, Bertha, indeed!"

"No, I am sure you would not. Mary, look across the room to where we were just now—to where my father is—my father, so compassionate and loving to me—and tell me what you see."

"I see," said Dot, who understood her well, "an old man sitting in a chair, and leaning sorrowfully on the back, with his face resting on his hand. As if his child should comfort him, Bertha."

"Yes, yes. She will. Go on."

"He is an old man worn with care and work. He is a spare, dejected, thoughtful, gray-haired man. I see him now, despondent and bowed down, and striving against nothing. But, Bertha, I have seen him many times before, and striving hard in many ways for one great sacred object. And I honor his gray head, and bless him!"

The Blind Girl broke away from her; and throwing herself upon her knees before him, took the gray head to her breast.

"It is my sight restored. It is my sight!" she cried. "I have been blind, and now my eyes are open. I never knew him! To think I might have died, and never truly seen the father who has been so loving to me!"

There were no words for Caleb's emotion.

"There is not a gallant figure on this earth," exclaimed the Blind Girl, holding him in her embrace, "that I would love so dearly, and would cherish so devotedly, as this! The grayer, and more worn, the dearer, father! Never let them say I am blind again. There's not a furrow in his face, there's not a hair upon his head, that shall be forgotten in my prayers and thanks to Heaven!"

Caleb managed to articulate "My Bertha!"

"And in my blindness, I believed him," said the girl caressing him with tears of exquisite affection, "to be so different!"

"The fresh smart father in the blue coat, Bertha," said poor Caleb. "He's gone!"

"Nothing is gone," she answered. "Dearest father, no! Everything is here—in you. The father that I loved so well; the father that I never loved enough, and never knew; All are here in you. Nothing is dead to me. The soul of all that was most dear to me is here—here, with the worn face, and the gray head. And I am NOT blind, father, any longer!"

Dot's whole attention had been concentrated, during this discourse, upon the father and daughter; but looking, now, towards the little Haymaker in the Moorish meadow, she saw the clock was within a few minutes of striking, and fell immediately, into a nervous and excited state.

"Father," said Bertha, hesitating. "Mary."

"Yes my dear," returned Caleb. "Here she is."

"There was no change in *her*. You never told me anything of *her* that was not true?"

"I should have done it my dear, I am afraid," returned Caleb, "if I could have made her better than she was. But I must have changed her for the worse, if I had changed her at all, Bertha."

Confident as the Blind Girl had been when she asked the question, her delight and pride in the reply and her renewed embrace of Dot, were charming to behold.

"More changes than you think for, may happen though, my dear," said Dot. "Changes for the better, I mean; changes for great joy to some of us. You musn't let them startle you too much, if any such should ever happen, and affect you? Are those wheels upon the road? You've a quick ear, Bertha. Are they wheels?"

"Yes. Coming very fast."

"I—I—I know you have a quick ear," said Dot, placing her hand upon her heart, and evidently talking on, as fast as she could, to hide its palpitating state, "because I have noticed it often, and because you were so quick to find out that strange step last night. Though why you should have said, as I very well recollect you did say, Bertha, 'Whose step is that!' and why you should have taken any greater observation of it than of any other step, I don't know. Though as I said just now, there are great changes in the world: great changes: and we can't do better than prepare ourselves to be surprised at hardly anything."

Caleb wondered what this meant; perceiving that she spoke to him, no less than to his daughter. He saw her, with astonishment, so fluttered and distressed that she could scarcely breathe; and holding to a chair, to save herself from falling.

"They are wheels indeed!" she panted, "Coming nearer! Nearer! Very close! And now you hear them stopping at the garden-gate! And now you hear a step outside the door—the same step, Bertha, is it not!—and now!"—

She uttered a wild cry of uncontrollable delight; and running up to Caleb put her hands upon his eyes, as a young man rushed into the room, and flinging away his hat into the air, came sweeping down upon them.

"Is it over?" cried Dot.

"Yes."

"Happily over?"

"Yes!"

"Do you recollect the voice, dear Caleb? Did you ever hear the like of it before?" cried Dot.

"If my boy in the Golden South Americas was alive"—said Caleb, trembling.

"He is alive!" shrieked Dot, removing her hands from his eyes, and clapping them in ecstasy; "look at him! See where he stands before you, healthy and strong! Your own dear son! Your own dear living, loving brother, Bertha!"

All honor to the little creature for her transports! All honor to her tears and laughter, when the three were locked in one another's arms! All honor to the heartiness with which she met the sunburnt sailor-fellow, with his dark streaming hair, half way, and never turned her rosy little mouth aside, but suffered him to kiss it, freely, and to press her to his bounding heart!

And honor to the Cuckoo too—why not!—for bursting out of the trap-door in the Moorish Palace like a housebreaker, and hiccoughing twelve times on the assembled company, as if he had got drunk for joy!

The Carrier, entering, started back. And well he might, to find himself in such good company.

"Look, John!" said Caleb, exultingly, "look here! My own boy from the Golden South Americas! My own son! Him that you fitted out, and sent away yourself! Him that you were always such a friend to!"

The Carrier advanced to seize him by the hand; but, recoiling, as some feature in his face awakened a remembrance of the Deaf Man in the Cart, said:

"Edward! Was it you?"

"Now tell him all!" cried Dot. "Tell him all, Edward; and don't spare me, for nothing shall make me spare myself in his eyes, ever again."

"I was the man," said Edward.

"And could you steal, disguised, into the house of your old friend?" rejoined the Carrier. "There was a frank boy once—how many years is it, Caleb, since we heard that he was dead, and had it proved, we thought?—who never would have done that."

"There was a generous friend of mind, once; more a father to me than a friend:" said Edward, "who never would have judged me, or any other man, unheard. You were he. So I am certain you will hear me now."

The Carrier, with a troubled glance at Dot, who still kept far away from him, replied, "Well! that's but fair. I will."

"You must know that when I left here, a boy," said Edward, "I was in love, and my love was returned. She was a very young girl, who perhaps (you may tell me) didn't know her own mind. But I knew mine, and I had a passion for her."

"You had!" exclaimed the Carrier. "You!"

"Indeed I had," returned the other. "And she returned it. I have ever since believed she did, and I am sure she did."

"Heaven help me!" said the Carrier. "This is worse than all."

"Constant to her," said Edward, "and returning, full of hope, after many hardships and perils, to redeem my part of our old contract, I heard, twenty miles away, that she was false to me; that she had forgotten me; and had bestowed herself upon another and a richer man. I had no mind to reproach her; but I wished to see her, and to prove beyond dispute that this was true. I hoped she might have been forced into it, against her own desire and recollection. It would be small comfort, but it would be some, I thought, and on I came. That I might have the truth, the real truth; observing freely for myself, and judging for myself, without obstruction on the one hand, or presenting my own influence (if I had any) before her, on the other; I dressed myself—unlike myself—you know how; and waited on the road—you know where. You had no suspicion of me;

neither had—had she," pointing to Dot, "until I whispered in her ear at that fireside, and she so nearly betrayed me."

"But when she knew that Edward was alive, and had come back," sobbed Dot, now speaking for herself, as she had burned to do all through this narrative: "and when she knew his purpose, she advised him by all means to keep his secret close; for his old friend John Peerybingle was much too open in his nature, and too clumsy in all artifice—being a clumsy man in general," said Dot, half laughing and half crying—"to keep it for him. And when she— that's me, John," sobbed the little woman—"told him all, and how his sweetheart had believed him to be dead; and how she had at last been over-persuaded by her mother into a marriage which the silly, dear old thing called advantageous; and when she—that's me again, John—told him they were not yet married (though close upon it), and that it would be nothing but a sacrifice if it went on, for there was no love on her side; and when he went nearly mad with joy to hear it; then she—that's me again—said she would go between them, as she had often done before in old times, John, and would sound his sweetheart and be sure that what she—me again, John—said and thought was right. And it WAS right, John! And they were brought together, John! And they were married, John, an hour ago! And here's the Bride! And Gruff and Tackleton may die a bachelor! And I'm a happy little woman, May, God bless you!"

She was an irresistible little woman, if that be anything to the purpose; and never so completely irresistible as in her present transports. There never were congratulations so endearing and delicious, as those she lavished on herself and on the Bride.

Amid the tumult of emotions in his breast, the honest Carrier had stood, confounded. Flying, now, towards her, Dot stretched out her hand to stop him, and retreated as before.

John was going to make another rush at this appeal; but she stopped him again.

"No John, no! Hear all! Don't love me any more, John, till you've heard every word I have to say. It was wrong to have a secret from you, John. I'm very sorry. I didn't think it any harm, till I came and sat down by you on the little stool last night. But when I knew by what was written in your face, that you had seen me walking in the gallery with Edward, and when I knew what you thought, I felt how giddy and how wrong it was. But oh, dear John, how could you, could you, think so!"

Little woman, how she sobbed again! John Peerybingle would have caught her in his arms. But no; she wouldn't let him.

"Don't you love me yet, please John! Not for a long time yet! When I was sad about this intended marriage, dear, it was because I remembered May and Edward such young lovers; and knew that her heart was far away from Tackleton. You believe that, now. Don't you John?"

John was going to make another rush at this appeal; but she stopped him again.

"No; keep there, please John! When I laugh at you, as I sometimes do, John, and call you clumsy and a dear old goose, and names of that sort, it's because I love you John, so well, and take such pleasure in your ways, and wouldn't see you altered in the least respect to have you made a King tomorrow."

"Hooroar!" said Caleb, with unusual vigor. "My opinion!"

"And when I speak of people being middle-aged, and steady, John, and pretend that we are a humdrum couple, going on in a jog-trot sort of way, it's only because I'm such a silly little thing, John, that I like, sometimes, to act a kind of Play with Baby, and all that: and make believe."

She saw that he was coming; and stopped him again. But she was very nearly too late.

"No, don't love me for another minute or two, if you please John! What I want most to tell you, I have kept to the last. My dear, good, generous John, when we were talking the other night about the Cricket, I had it on my lips to say, that at first I did not love you quite so dearly as I do now; that when I first came home here, I was half afraid I mightn't learn to love you every bit as well as I hoped and prayed I might—being so very young, John! But, dear John,

every day and hour I loved you more and more. And if I could
have loved you better than I do, the noble words I heard you say
this morning, would have made me. But I can't. All the affection
that I had (it was a great deal John) I gave you, as you well deserve,
long, long ago, and I have no more left to give. Now, my dear
husband, take me to your heart again! That's my home, John; and
never, never think of sending me to any other!"

But, now, the sound of wheels was heard again outside the door;
and somebody exclaimed that Gruff and Tackleton was coming
back. Speedily that worthy gentleman appeared, looking warm
and flustered.

"Why, what the Devil's this, John Peerybingle!" said Tackleton.
"There's some mistake, I appointed Mrs. Tackleton to meet me at
the church, and I'll swear I passed her on the road, on her way here.
Oh! here she is! I beg your pardon, sir; I haven't the pleasure of
knowing you; but if you can do me the favor to spare this young
lady, she has rather a particular engagement this morning."

"But I can't spare her," returned Edward. "I couldn't think of it."

"What do you mean, you vagabond?" said Tackleton.

"I mean, that as I can make allowance for your being vexed,"
returned the other with a smile, "I am as deaf to harsh discourse
this morning, as I was to all discourse last night."

The look that Tackleton bestowed upon him, and the start he gave!

"I am sorry, sir," said Edward, holding out May's left hand and
especially the third finger; "that the young lady can't accompany
you to church; but as she has been there once, this morning, perhaps you'll excuse her."

Tackleton looked hard at the third finger, and took a little piece
of silver paper, apparently containing a ring, from his waistcoat-
pocket.

"Miss Slowboy," said Tackleton. "Will you have the kindness to
throw that in the fire? Thank'ee."

"It was a previous engagement, quite an old engagement, that prevented my wife from keeping her appointment with you, I assure you," said Edward.

"Mr. Tackleton will do me the justice to acknowledge that I revealed it to him faithfully, and that I told him, many times I never could forget it," said May blushing.

"Oh certainly!" said Tackleton. "Oh to be sure. Oh it's all right. It's quite correct. Mrs. Edward Plummer, I infer?"

"That's the name," returned the bridegroom.

"Ah, I shouldn't have known you sir," said Tackleton, scrutinizing his face narrowly, and making a low bow. "I give you joy sir!"

"Thank'ee."

"Mrs. Peerybingle," said Tackleton, turning suddenly to where she stood with her husband; "I am sorry. You haven't done me a very great kindness, but upon my life I am sorry. You are better than I thought you. John Peerybingle, I am sorry. You understand me; that's enough. It's quite correct, ladies and gentlemen all, and perfectly satisfactory. Good-morning!"

With these words he carried it off, and carried himself off too: merely stopping at the door, to take the flowers and favors from his horse's head, and to kick that animal once, in the ribs, as a means of informing him that there was a screw loose in his arrangements.

Of course it became a serious duty now, to make such a day of it, as should mark these events for a high Feast and Festival in the Peerybingle Calendar for evermore.

Then, there was a great Expedition set on foot to go and find out Mrs. Fielding; and to be dismally penitent to that excellent gentlewoman; and to bring her back, by force, if needful, to be happy and forgiving. And when the Expedition first discovered her, she would listen to no terms at all, but said, an unspeakable number of times, that ever she should have lived to see the day! and couldn't be got to say anything else, except, "Now carry me to the grave:" which seemed absurd, on account of her not being dead, or anything at all like it. After a time, she lapsed into a state of dreadful calmness, and observed, that when that unfortunate train of circumstances had occurred in the Indigo Trade, she had forseen that she would be exposed, during her whole life, to every species of insult and contumely; and that she was glad to find it was the case; and begged they wouldn't trouble themselves about her—for what was she? oh, dear! a nobody!—but would forget that such a being lived, and would take their course in life without her. From this bitterly sarcastic mood, she passed into an angry one, in which she gave vent to the remarkable expression that the worm would turn if trodden on; and, after that, she yielded to a soft regret, and said, if they had only given her their confidence, what might she not have had it in her power to suggest! Taking advantage of this crisis in her feelings, the Expedition embraced her; and she very soon had her gloves on, and was on her way to John Peerybingle's in a state of unimpeachable gentility.

After dinner, Caleb sang the song about the Sparkling Bowl. As I'm a living man, hoping to keep so, for a year or two, he sang it through.

And, by the bye, a most unlooked-for incident occurred, just as he finished the last verse.

There was a tap at the door; and a man came staggering in, without saying with your leave, or by your leave, with something heavy on his head. Setting this down in the middle of the table, symmetrically in the centre of the nuts and apples, he said:

"Mr. Tackleton's compliments, and as he hasn't got no use for the cake himself, p'raps you'll eat it."

And with those words, he walked off.

There was some surprise among the company, as you may imagine. Mrs. Fielding, being a lady of infinite discernment, suggested that the cake was poisoned, and related a narrative of a cake, which, within her knowledge, had turned a seminary for young ladies, blue. But she was overruled by acclamation; and the cake was cut by May, with much ceremony and rejoicing.

I don't think any one had tasted it, when there came another tap at the door, and the same man appeared again, having under his arm a vast brown paper parcel.

"Mr. Tackleton's compliments, and he'd sent a few toys for the Babby. They an't ugly."

After the delivery of which expressions, he retired again.

The whole party would have experienced great difficulty in finding words for their astonishment, even if they had had ample time to seek them. But, they had none at all; for, the messenger had scarcely shut the door behind him, when there came another tap, and Tackleton himself walked in.

"Mrs. Peerybingle!" said the Toy-merchant, hat in hand. "I'm sorry. I'm more sorry than I was this morning. I have had time to think of it. John Peerybingle! I'm sour by disposition; but I can't help being sweetened, more or less, by coming face to face with such a man as you. Caleb! This unconscious little nurse gave me a broken hint last night, of which I have found the thread. I blush to think how easily I might have bound you and your daughter to me, and what a miserable idiot I was, when I took her for one! Friends, one and all, my house is very lonely to-night. I have not so much as a Cricket on the Hearth. I have scared them all away. Be gracious to me; let me join this happy party!"

He was at home in five minutes. You never saw such a fellow. What *had* he been doing with himself all his life, never to have known, before, his great capacity of being jovial! Or what had the Fairies been doing with him, to have effected such a change!

"John! you won't send me home this evening; will you?" whispered Dot.

There was a dance in the evening.

May and Edward got up, amid great applause, to dance alone; and Bertha plays her liveliest tune.

Well! if you'll believe me, they have not been dancing five minutes, when suddenly the Carrier flings his pipe away, takes Dot round the waist, dashes out into the room, and starts off with her, toe and heel, quite wonderfully. Tackelton no sooner sees this, than he skims across to Mrs. Fielding, takes her round the waist, and follows suit. Caleb no sooner sees this, than he clutches Tilly Slowboy by both hands and goes off at score; Miss Slowboy, firm in the belief that diving hotly in among the other couples, and effecting any number of concussions with them, is your only principle of footing it.

Hark! how the Cricket joins the music with its Chirp, Chirp, Chirp; and how the kettle hums!

*   *   *   *   *

But what is this! Even as I listen to them, blithely, and turn towards Dot, for one last glimpse of a little figure very pleasant to me, she and the rest have vanished into air, and I am left alone. A Cricket sings upon the Hearth; a broken child's-toy lies upon the ground; and nothing else remains.

A Child's
Dream
of a
Star

Again the child dreamed of the open star, and of the company of angels,
and the train of people.

There was once a child, and he strolled about a good deal, and thought of a number of things. He had a sister, who was a child too, and his constant companion. These two used to wonder all day long. They wondered at the beauty of the flowers; they wondered at the height and blueness of the sky; they wondered at the depth of the bright water; they wondered at the goodness and power of GOD who made the world.

They used to say to one another, sometimes, Supposing all the children upon the earth were to die, would the flowers, and the water, and the sky be sorry? They believed they would be sorry. For, said they, the buds are the children of the flowers, and the little playful streams that gambol down the hill-sides are the children of the water; and the smallest bright specks playing at hide and seek in the sky all night, must surely be the children of the stars; and they would all be grieved to see their playmates, the children of men, no more.

There was one clear shining star that used to come out in the sky before the rest, near the church spire, above the graves. It was larger and more beautiful, they thought, than all the others, and every night they watched for it, standing hand in hand at a window. Whoever saw it first cried out, "I see the star!" And often they cried out both together, knowing so well when it would rise, and where. So they grew to be such friends with it, that, before lying down in their beds, they always looked out once again, to bid it good-night; and when they were turning round to sleep, they used to say, "God bless the star!"

But while she was still very young, oh very very young, the sister drooped, and came to be so very weak that she could no longer stand in the window at night; and then the child looked sadly out by himself, and when he saw the star, turned round and said to the patient pale face on the bed, "I see the star!" and then a smile would come upon the face, and a little weak voice used to say, "God bless my brother and the star!"

And so the time came all too soon! when the child looked out alone, and when there was no face on the bed; and when there was a little grave among the graves, not there before; and when the star made long rays down towards him, as he saw it through his tears.

Now, these rays were so bright, and they seemed to make such a shining way from earth to Heaven, that when the child went to his solitary bed, he dreamed about the star; and dreamed that, lying where he was, he saw a train of people taken up that sparkling road by angels. And the star, opening, showed him a great world of light, where many more such angels waited to receive them.

All these angels, who were waiting, turned their beaming eyes upon the people who were carried up into the star; and some came out from the long rows in which they stood, and fell upon the people's necks, and kissed them tenderly, and went away with them down avenues of light, and were so happy in their company, that lying in his bed he wept for joy.

But, there were many angels who did not go with them, and among them one he knew. The patient face that once had lain upon the bed was glorified and radiant, but his heart found out his sister among all the host.

His sister's angel lingered near the entrance of the star, and said to the leader among those who had brought the people thither:

"Is my brother come?"

And he said "No."

She was turning hopefully away, when the child stretched out his arms, and cried, "O, sister, I am here! Take me!" and then she turned her beaming eyes upon him, and it was night; and the star was shining in the room, making long rays down towards him as he saw it through his tears.

From that hour forth, the child looked out upon the star as on the home he was to go to, when his time should come; and he thought that he did not belong to the earth alone, but to the star too, because of his sister's angel gone before.

There was a baby born to be a brother to the child; and while he was so little that he never yet had spoken a word, he stretched his tiny form out on his bed, and died.

Again the child dreamed of the open star, and of the company of angels, and the train of people, and the rows of angels with their beaming eyes all turned upon those people's faces.

Said his sister's angel to the leader:

"Is my brother come?"

And he said, "Not that one, but another."

As the child beheld his brother's angel in her arms, he cried, "O, sister, I am here! Take me!" And she turned and smiled upon him, and the star was shining.

He grew to be a young man, and was busy at his books when an old servant came to him and said:

"Thy mother is no more. I bring her blessing on her darling son!"

Again at night he saw the star, and all that former company. Said his sister's angel to the leader:

"Is my brother come?"

And he said, "Thy mother!"

A mighty cry of joy went forth through all the star, because the mother was re-united to her two children. And he stretched out his arms and cried, "O, mother, sister and brother, I am here! Take me!" And they answered him, "Not yet," and the star was shining.

He grew to be a man, whose hair was turning gray, and he was sitting in his chair by the fireside, heavy with grief, and with his face bedewed with tears, when the star opened once again.

Said his sister's angel to the leader: "Is my brother come?"

And he said, "Nay, but his maiden daughter."

And the man who had been the child saw his daughter, newly lost to him, a celestial creature among those three, and he said, "My daughter's head is on my sister's bosom, and her arm is around my mother's neck, and at her feet there is the baby of old time, and I can bear the parting from her, GOD be praised!"

And the star was shining.

Thus the child came to be an old man, and his once smooth face was wrinkled, and his steps were slow and feeble, and his back was bent. And one night as he lay upon his bed, his children standing round, he cried, as he had cried so long ago:

"I see the star!"

They whispered to one another, "He is dying."

And he said, "I am. My age is falling from me like a garment, and I move towards the star as a child. And O, my Father, now I thank thee that it has so often opened, to receive those dear ones who await me!"

And the star was shining; and it shines upon his grave.

A
New Year's
Gift

*"This is your first New Year's Day in England," he said. "Will you let
me help to make it like a New Year's Day at home?"*

New Year's Day, among the English, is associated with the giving and receiving of dinners, and with nothing more. New Year's
Day, among the foreigners, is the grand opportunity of the year for the giving and receiving of presents. It is occasionally possible
to acclimatise a foreign custom. In this instance Vendale felt no
hesitation about making the attempt. His one difficulty was to
decide what his New Year's gift to Marguerite should be. The
defensive pride of the peasant's daughter—morbidly sensitive to
the inequality between her social position and his—would be secretly roused against him if he ventured on a rich offering. A gift,
which a poor man's purse might purchase, was the one gift that
could be trusted to find its way to her heart, for the giver's sake.
Stoutly resisting temptation, in the form of diamonds and rubies,
Vendale bought a brooch of the filigree-work of Genoa—the sim-
plest and most unpretending ornament that he could find in the
jeweller's shop.

He slipped his gift into Marguerite's hand as she held it out to welcome him on the day of the dinner.

"This is your first New Year's Day in England," he said. "Will you let me help to make it like a New Year's Day at home?"

She thanked him, a little constrainedly, as she looked at the jeweller's box, uncertain what it might contain. Opening the box, and discovering the studiously simple form under which Vendale's little keepsake offered itself to her, she penetrated his motive on the spot. Her face turned on him brightly, with a look which said, "I own you have pleased and flattered me." Never had she been so charming, in Vendale's eyes, as she was at that moment.—*from "No Thoroughfare"*

The Life
of
Our Lord

I have always striven in my writings to express veneration for the life and lessons of our Saviour; because I feel it; and because I re-wrote that history for my children—every one of whom knew it, from having it repeated to them, long before they could read, and almost as soon as they could speak.—from a letter, 1870

I commit my soul to the mercy of God through our Lord and Saviour Jesus Christ, and I exhort my dear children humbly to try to guide themselves by the teaching of the New Testament in its broad spirit, and to put no faith in any man's narrow construction of its letter here or there.—from Dickens's last Will and Testament, May 12, 1869

 Chapter the First

My dear children, I am very anxious that you should know something about the History of Jesus Christ. For everybody ought to know about Him. No one ever lived, who was so good, so kind, so gentle, and so sorry for all people who did wrong, or were in anyway miserable, as he was. And as he is now in Heaven, where we hope to go, and all to meet each other after we are dead, and there be happy always together, you never can think what a good place Heaven is, without knowing who he was and what he did.

He was born, a long long time ago—nearly Two Thousand years ago—at a place called Bethlehem. His father and mother lived in a city called Nazareth, but they were forced, by business to travel to Bethlehem. His father's name was Joseph, and his mother's name was Mary. And the town being very full of people, also brought there by business, there was no room for Joseph and Mary in the inn or in any house; so they went into a Stable to lodge, and in this stable Jesus Christ was born. There was no cradle or anything of that kind there, so Mary laid her pretty little boy in what is called the Manger, which is the place the horses eat out of. And there he fell asleep.

While he was asleep, some Shepherds who were watching Sheep in the Fields, saw an Angel from God, all light and beautiful, come moving over the grass towards Them. At first they were afraid and fell down and hid their faces. But it said "There is a child born to-day in the city of Bethlehem near here, who will grow up to be so good that God will love him as his own son; and he will teach men to love one another, and not to quarrel and hurt one another; and his name will be Jesus Christ; and people will put that name in their prayers, because they will know God loves it, and will know that they should love it too." And then the Angel told the Shepherds to go to that Stable, and look at that little child in the Manger. Which they did; and they kneeled down by it in its sleep, and said "God bless this child!"

Now the great place of all that country was Jerusalem—just as London is the great place in England—and at Jerusalem the King lived, whose name was King Herod. Some wise men came one day, from a country a long way off in the East, and said to the King "We have seen a Star in the sky, which teaches us to know that a child is born in Bethlehem who will live to be a man whom all people will love." When King Herod heard this, he was jealous, for he was a wicked man. But he pretended not to be, and said to the wise men, "Whereabouts is this child?" And the wise men said "We don't know. But we think the Star will shew us; for the Star has been moving on before us, all the way here, and is now standing still in the sky." Then Herod asked them to see if the Star would shew them where the child lived, and ordered them, if they found the child, to come back to him. So they went out, and the Star went on, over their heads a little way before them, until it stopped over the house where the child was. This was very wonderful, but God ordered it to be so.

When the Star stopped, the wise men went in, and saw the child with Mary his Mother. They loved him very much, and gave him some presents. Then they went away. But they did not go back to King Herod; for they thought he was jealous, though he had not said so. So they went away, by night, back into their own country. And an Angel came, and told Joseph and Mary to take the child into a Country called Egypt, or Herod would kill him. So they escaped too, in the night—the father, the mother, and the child— and arrived there, safely.

But when this cruel Herod found that the wise men did not come back to him, and that he could not, therefore, find out where this child, Jesus Christ, lived, he called his soldiers and captains to him, and told them to go and Kill all the children in his dominions that were not more than two years old. The wicked men did so. The mothers of the children ran up and down the streets with them in their arms trying to save them, and hide them in caves and cellars, but it was of no use. The soldiers with their swords killed all the children they could find. This dreadful murder was called the Murder of the Innocents. Because the little children were so innocent.

King Herod hoped that Jesus Christ was one of them. But He was not, as you know, for He had escaped safely into Egypt. And he lived there, with his father and mother, until Bad King Herod died.

Chapter the Second

When King Herod was dead, an angel came to Joseph again, and said he might now go to Jerusalem, and not be afraid for the child's sake. So Joseph and Mary, and her Son Jesus Christ (who are commonly called the Holy Family) travelled towards Jerusalem; but hearing on the way that King Herod's son was the new King, and fearing that he, too, might want to hurt the child, they turned out of the way, and went to live in Nazareth. They lived there, until Jesus Christ was twelve years old.

Then Joseph and Mary went to Jerusalem to attend a Religious Feast which used to be held in those days, in the Temple of Jerusalem, which was a great church or Cathedral; and they took Jesus Christ with them. And when the Feast was over, they travelled away from Jerusalem, back towards their own home in Nazareth, with a great many of their friends and neighbours. For people used, then, to travel a great many together, for fear of robbers; the roads not being so safe and well guarded as they are now, and travelling being much more difficult altogether, than it now is.

They travelled on, for a whole day, and never knew that Jesus Christ was not with them; for the company being so large, they thought he was somewhere among the people, though they did not see Him. But finding that he was not there, and fearing that he was lost, they turned back to Jerusalem in great anxiety to look for him. They found him, sitting in the Temple, talking about the goodness of God, and how we should all pray to him, with some learned men who were called Doctors. They were not what you understand by the word "doctors" now; they did not attend sick people; they were scholars and clever men. And Jesus Christ shewed such knowledge in what he said to them, and in the questions he asked them, that they were all astonished.

He went, with Joseph and Mary, home to Nazareth, when they had found him, and lived there until he was thirty or thirty-five years old.

There cannot be many men, I believe, who have a more humble venera-tion for the New Testament, or a more profound conviction of its all-sufficiency, than I have. If I am ever (as you tell me I am) mistaken on this subject, it is because I discountenance all obtrusive professions of and tradings in religion, as one of the main causes why real Christi-anity has been retarded in this world; and because my observation of life induces me to hold in unspeakable dread and horror, those un-seemly squabbles about the letter which drive the spirit out of hun-dreds of thousands.—from a letter, 1856

The Dickens
Family
Prayers

Prayer at Night

Lord our heavenly Father, almighty and everlasting God, who in thy inestimable goodness hast directed and preserved us during the past day, and brought us to another night surrounded by such great blessings and instances of thy mercy, we beseech thee to hear our heartfelt thanks for all the benefits we enjoy, and our humble prayers that we may cheerfully endeavour every day of our lives to be in some degree more worthy their possession. Sanctify and improve to us any good thought that has been presented to us in any form during this day; forgive us the sins we have committed during its progress and in our past lives; all the wrong we have done; and all the negligences and ignorances of which we have been guilty; and enable us to find in any trials we have undergone or sorrows we have known, or have yet to experience, blessed instructions for our future happiness.

We humbly pray almighty Father for our dear children, that thou wilt vouchsafe to watch over and preserve them from all danger and evil; for ourselves that thou wilt prolong our lives and health and energies and success for many years, for their dear sakes; and for them and us, that thou wilt grant us cheerfulness of spirit—tranquility and contentment. That we may be honest and true in all our dealings, and gentle and merciful to the faults of others: remembering of how much gentleness and mercy we stand in need ourselves. That we may earnestly try to live in thy true faith, honour and love, and in charity and goodwill with all our fellow creatures. That we may worship thee in every beautiful and wonderful thing thou hast made; and sympathize with the whole world of thy glorious creation. Grant that in the contemplation of thy wisdom and goodness, and in reverence for our Lord Jesus Christ, we may endeavour to do our duty, in those stations of life in which it pleases thee to call us, and be held together in a bond of affection and mutual love which no change or lapse of time can weaken; which shall sustain and teach us to do right in all reverses of good or evil; and which shall comfort and console us most, when we most require support, by filling us, in the hour of sickness and death, with a firm reliance on thee, and the assurance that through thy great mercy we shall meet again in another and happy state of existence beyond the grave, where care and grief and parting are unknown, and where we shall be once again united to the dear friends lost to us on this earth.

Pardon, gracious God, the imperfections of our prayers and thanks, and read them in our hearts rather than in these feeble and imperfect words. Hear our supplications in behalf of the poor, the sick, the destitute and guilty, and for thy blessing on the diffusion of increased happiness, knowledge, and comfort among the great mass of mankind, that they may not be tempted to the commission of crimes which, in want and man's neglect, it is hard to resist. Bless and keep our dear children, and all those who are nearest and dearest to us; and by thy help and our Saviour's teaching, enable us to lay our heads upon our pillows every night, at peace with all the world. And may his grace and thy love and the fellowship of thy Holy Spirit be with us all evermore. Amen.

The Children's Prayer

Pray God who has made everything and is so kind and merciful to everything he has made: pray God to bless my dear Papa and Mama, brothers and sisters and all my relations and friends: make me a good little child and let me never be naughty and tell a lie, which is a mean and shameful thing. Make me kind to my nurses and servants and to all beggars and poor people and let me never be cruel to any dumb creature; and pray God to bless and preserve us all this night and for ever, for the sake of Jesus Christ, our Lord. Amen.

I don't know what to do!" cried Scrooge, laughing and crying in the same breath . . . "I am as light as a feather, I am as happy as an angel, I am as merry as a schoolboy. I am as giddy as a drunken man. A merry Christmas to everybody! A happy New Year to all the world!"
A Christmas Carol

"God bless Us, Every One!"
A Christmas Carol